Acknowledgements

Many thanks must go to all of ███████████ ...ot so young, who have given ███████████ ...ent, support, and friendship while An. ███ ...thrashing around in my head. I am grateful to the help I received from editors Freda Nobbs and Dawn Loewen, and especially from Diane Morriss, Sono Nis Press publisher, who made getting this book into print such an easy family-feeling kind of collaboration. Without your enthusiasm and warmth the whole process would not have been such an absolute pleasure.

Thanks to Linda Lee Crosfield, a first-rate editor, for helping me sharpen my quill and for providing my border collie, Shira, with a safe and loving "home away from home."

Many thanks to the following people for all their help: Linda Murray for teaching Shira and me how to play together and respect each other. To Jennifer Craig for dog-sitting Shira any time I needed a place to drop her off. To Sally MacKenzie for allowing me to hang out at a GETT camp. To Laura Campese and Nicole Koehle for the use of their GETT camp group name, The Steel Toes. To Anona Zmur for her information on mental illnesses.

Author's Note: Because of constant changes in knowledge about mental illnesses, some of the information about schizophrenia may soon be out of date.

In loving memory of my Oma, Anne Marie Poelma. Also to Mies (Maria) Braal, Helen Stevenson, Ruth Wolfe, and all grandparents who live by good example.

Summer of Changes

SUMMER of changes

ANN ALMA

sononis

WINLAW, BRITISH COLUMBIA

NATIONAL LIBRARY OF CANADA CATALOGUING IN PUBLICATION DATA

Alma, Ann, 1946-
    Summer of changes

    (Summer series)
    ISBN 1-55039-120-8

    I. Title. II. Series: Alma, Ann, 1946- Summer series.
PS8551.L565S85 2001   jC813'.54 C2001-911138-X
PZ7.A444Su 2001

Sono Nis Press most gratefully acknowledges the support for our publishing program provided by the Government of Canada through the Book Publishing Industry Development Program (BPIDP), The Canada Council for the Arts, and the British Columbia Arts Council.

First Printing: September 2001
Second Printing: November 2002

Edited by Freda Nobbs and Dawn Loewen
Cover design by Jim Brennan

Published by
SONO NIS PRESS
Box 160
Winlaw, B.C. V0G 2J0
1-800-370-5228
sononis@islandnet.com
www.islandnet.com/sononis/

Distributed in the U.S. by
Orca Book Publishers
Box 468
Custer, WA 98240-0468
1-800-210-5277

Printed and bound in Canada
by Houghton Boston Printing.

The Canada Council | Le Conseil des Arts
for the Arts | du Canada

CHAPTER 1

Ignoring the screeching protest of the rusty hinges, Anneke opened the door to the cave. Stale, musty air greeted her nostrils. She stepped inside and, without turning, called to the boy standing behind her, "Come in."

Ken hesitated, his chunky body filling most of the small entrance.

"I have candles," Anneke said proudly.

"It smells funny." He stayed in the doorway.

"This is an old root cellar. It was built a long time ago." Anneke moved around quickly in the semi-darkness, putting two chunks of wood into place as seats.

"It's creepy," Ken said.

"Well, if you're scared, then leave," Anneke scoffed, running her hands through her short, brown hair. She sat down on one chunk of wood, put a cookie on an upside-down pail in the middle of the cave, and ate one herself. Sheera, her black and white border collie, sat on a mat beside her and crunched noisily on a dog biscuit.

Ken touched the big boulders in the wall of the cave as if he thought they might tumble down. When the massive rocks didn't move, he took a step inside, touched one of the boulders again, then rubbed his hands together as if to clean them. Sitting on the edge of her chunk of wood, Anneke pointed to the extra cookie. Ken took it between the tips of his fingers and nibbled at the edge. They stared at each other in silence for a while, his black eyes meeting her defiant blue eyes, before Ken said, "My mom doesn't know I'm here. It's almost dinner-time."

"Come back only when you're invited." While Anneke watched him leave, she wondered if she should have asked this boy from down the road over at all. So far the cave had been only hers and Sheera's.

Blowing out the candle and slamming the door shut behind her, she said to her dog, "Let's make macaroni and cheese for you and me and Mother." They ran down the hill, through a field of tall summer weeds, and to the back door of an old trailer. Kicking off her shoes and leaving them where they fell, Anneke walked in.

"Hi, Mother," she said, looking at a woman standing on her head in the middle of the living room. Long, red hair lay spread around her like a mat. Her hands were placed flat on the floor while her elbows stuck out at sharp angles. Spindly legs, in bright red long johns, stuck straight up into the air.

"Hi, honey." The woman stayed upside down. In a low voice she chanted, "Ohhhmmm, ohhhmmm." The frilly white lace she had sewn onto the bottom of the long underwear and onto the sleeves of her red top quivered from time to time. Her left cheek and eye twitched. Otherwise she was still.

Anneke made dinner and fed Sheera. She gave a plate of food to her mother who by now was seated on one of their three straight-backed chairs. They watched TV as they ate. Anneke wondered why Mother always liked these silly game shows, the ones with bells and spinning dials. Mother cheered, her mouth full, every time the TV audience cheered. Anneke just chewed and swallowed, waiting for the sitcoms to start in a few hours. She could do her homework while the game shows were on but decided to leave the math until the next morning. She'd finish the multiplication questions then. Watching Mother, who had put her empty plate on the floor for Sheera to lick, Anneke couldn't help but giggle. Mother really loved to see people win things—she clapped her hands a lot. Anneke moved her chair closer to Mother, who put an arm around her shoulder. She cheered along, a silly grin on her face.

In the morning Anneke felt tired. They hadn't gone to bed until almost midnight and now there was no time to finish the homework.

"Do it later," Mother yawned.

"I'll probably get in trouble, like yesterday, and the day before." Anneke sighed and put her peanut butter sandwich in her school bag. "Don't forget to eat lunch," she told her mother.

Of course Mr. Brownwig, her grade five teacher, made her stay after school again. It was a good thing there were only three more weeks of torture left before the summer holidays. Finishing the math just in time, she rushed out to the bus and ended up with a seat in the front, right behind the driver. Ken sat in the back with the big kids. He was one of the smarter and older boys in her class. Anneke remembered that he had turned eleven several months ago. Even though she was taller than he was, Anneke had turned eleven only a few weeks ago.

When the bus dropped her off, she jogged down the road to the trailer, threw her school bag into the mudroom, and yelled, "I'm home." When there was no answer she stuck her head around the living room door and peeked in. As often happened, her mother was not there. But Sheera stood just inside the door, her tail wagging.

"What are you doing in here alone?" she asked, hugging her pet.

Sheera whined happily as they went out. The dog ran up the hill in the direction of the cave, then back, wanting Anneke to follow her.

"Yes, yes, I'm coming," Anneke puffed as she reached the top of the hill. "Slow down, you silly mutt." She frowned when she saw the plastic pail outside the cave door. Shoving the door open, she froze at the entrance as a cloud of smoke belched out, engulfing her. Where the upside-down pail used to be, a small pile of twigs smouldered. A shadow, dressed all in black, jumped in her direction. Sheera growled. Anneke breathed in sharply, then put her hands on her hips and stayed where she was.

"Beware," a shrill voice called. "Beware of evil. Beware." Black arms waved in her direction.

"Mother!" Anneke said in a loud, stern voice, rushing inside to grab the smoking twigs and throw them out. As she bent down, her mother's hands clasped her wrists.

"Beware. They will come to chain us."

"Mother, let go. That's enough." Loosening the woman's grip on her, Anneke threw the branches outside and waved Sheera's mat back and forth to try to clear some of the smoke. "Come on." She took her mother's hand and led her outside. The hand shook, the long, thin fingers lying limply in her own strong grip.

Anneke brought out two stumps and they sat in the heat of the late-afternoon June air. She hadn't realized that her mother knew this place existed. She wanted it to be *her* hideaway, just hers and Sheera's, and maybe Ken's when she wanted him to come over.

Her mother, now calmer, breathed deeply, coughed, and spat on the ground. She rested her head on her daughter's shoulder, her troubled eyes closed against the sun, her left cheek and eye twitching.

"Did you take your medication?"

The woman nodded briefly. "I think so," she mumbled.

"If you don't take it, you know what will happen. They'll put you back in a hospital. Or in a group home. You don't like that." Anneke slid one arm around her mother's shoulder. Mother sighed.

"And I don't want to go to a foster home again. You have to be normal."

Again a sigh, no other response. Sheera put her head on Anneke's knee and stared up at her. While she absently petted Sheera, Anneke frowned. She needed to keep track of Mother's medication more carefully. If her mother took a pill every day, she could control her schizophrenia and lead a normal life. The doctor had said so three years ago, when Anneke moved from her foster home back to living with her mother.

"How did you find the cave?" she asked.

Her mother looked up. "The goddess told me about it. She steered me to her, to rest in her."

A tear dropped onto Anneke's shirt. She didn't mind her mother's crying. Tears were calmer, and even sobs were easier than raging and screaming. When Mother cried, she listened better.

"Why did you make a fire?"

"To clean my soul. But I got scared. Evil filled the room. There's evil, evil." Mother's eyes became wilder again.

"You need your medication." Anneke stood up and, holding her mother's hand firmly, led her down the hill. In the kitchen she made her swallow one of the pills the doctor had prescribed and put her to bed.

Anneke turned the TV on and watched a few minutes of a game show, then decided watching alone was boring. She jumped up and rolled on the floor with Sheera for a while. "Shhh," she whispered when the dog barked excitedly. "Mother's sleeping."

Maybe Ken would come over again. They could sit outside in the sun in front of the cave. They could build a porch onto the front of the cave. Maybe Ken could be her friend. He was the only other student who got off at the same bus stop as Anneke. They could play together, outside only, not in each other's places. Anneke didn't have any friends. She was afraid to bring anyone here because of Mother. Ken didn't usually play with anyone, either. He always sat with his nose in a book while he ate his unusual lunches. She'd heard someone call him "Riceball." No one called her names—no one talked to her at all. But yesterday on the bus he'd said yes, he'd come over. He had even seemed excited about it. And he would never need to meet Mother.

With Sheera in the lead, Anneke ran down their road, past trailers like the one she lived in, past clusters of small houses, until they came to a large, two-storey house.

Ken's home sat in the middle of a well-kept lawn, which was cut as short and even as his black hair. Anneke's yard was full of tall weeds, but here at Ken's, small shrubs grew in pots by the windows. Flowers bloomed in strips along the path from the sidewalk to the house, and two butterflies fluttered from blossom to blossom. On one side the yard had big rocks and gravel raked around a Japanese stone lantern. Not even a tiny weed showed anywhere.

Anneke leaned on the gate. She'd never gone past this point. Then she shrugged and walked through the gate and down the path. She reached for the bell just as Ken opened the door.

"Do you want to help me build a porch at my cave?" she asked.

Ken shuffled his slippered feet on the shiny floor. "I have to ask my mom." He disappeared.

Anneke looked at the hallway, with a row of shiny coat hooks on one wall and pairs of slippers, exactly side by side, under them. Against the opposite wall stood a big, green plant with a huge mirror on one side and a colourful stained-glass window on the other. On a shelf sat a row of Japanese dolls dressed in kimonos. This place was sure different from Anneke's own built-on mudroom, full of boxes, a garbage can, and a jumble of coats, hats, and shoes all thrown onto the floor in one corner.

"OK." Ken put his slippers beside the others. He carried his shoes to the door before putting them on.

At the cave he held each of four posts in turn while Anneke tied them with ropes to rocks or tree trunks. Then she nailed a board on top while Ken held the posts again.

He wiped his forehead. "You're good at carpentry," he said admiringly. "I could never do all this."

"There's not much to it," Anneke said. "I plan to live here quite a bit in the summer."

"It's too hot outside and too cold in there," Ken replied, pointing to the cave. "This porch is cool though."

Anneke sat down in the shade. "People called Doukhobors used to store their vegetables in here. It never freezes. It's always the same temperature, summer or winter, because it's underground."

Ken looked at the dark hollow. "Doukhobors," he mumbled.

"Yes, you know, the people who came here from Russia a long time ago. They had a communal house around here. They grew apples and other fruit right on these hills." Anneke waved her arm around.

"I know," Ken said. "My neighbour is a Doukhobor. She gives us vegetables from her garden. She cooks borscht sometimes and homemade bread—"

"I could cook things here," Anneke interrupted. "I'll get a little stove.

"Won't your mom—" Ken stopped.

Anneke shrugged and didn't reply. When had come back from her foster home and started living with Mother again, she'd decided not to talk to anyone about her home life. "A cozy little stove," she said. "You can come here for dinner sometime."

"My mom doesn't . . ." He shrugged. "I stay home a lot to read."

Anneke scratched her leg. "I'm up here most of the time. With Sheera."

They sat silently in the shade, until Anneke said, "I never feel lonely because I have my dog."

"Lucky," Ken sighed. Then he brightened. "I'm never really lonely either. I have my books." He looked at his watch. "I have to go. We were supposed to eat soon. I told Mom we would just go for a walk. I'm not supposed to—" He looked down. "She likes me to get exercise, though."

"Come back tomorrow if you want," Anneke called as he ran down the hill.

"I will," he yelled back over his shoulder.

"Let's see what we can find for food," she said, racing Sheera to the trailer. They found Mother in the kitchen, singing along with a song on the radio.

"Hi, honey," she said, giving her daughter a hug.

Lids played a rhythm on steaming pots as delicious smells filled the air. Mother knew beans and sausages were Anneke's favourite dinner.

Anneke carried an old piece of black pipe to the cave. In two weeks the summer holidays would start, and she wanted to have a stove in place by then. So today after school she'd walked to the garbage dump and had crawled under a loose piece of fence onto the site. While the dump attendant was busy elsewhere, Anneke had searched the back of the lot, the weedy part where the workers stored odds and ends, things that had been thrown away but that were too good to be burned. Sometimes people looked around here and found just what they needed. They'd bargain with the attendant and take their new treasure home for a few dollars. But Anneke had no money. She had found the piece of pipe right away and had leaned it against the fence. Scrounging around some more for a stove, she saw old rolls of wire, bed springs, a bathtub, chairs, a table with a broken leg, windows and more windows, doors, tires on rims, and a baby's highchair, but no stove. When the attendant had turned from the far end of the dump and come in her direction, she'd hidden behind the doors until he disappeared into his shack. Then she'd taken the pipe and left.

Now Anneke set her treasure against one of the porch posts. Taking a key ring from her belt, she unlocked the new padlock she'd put on the cave's door yesterday. With the door locked, the place really belonged to her. The cave had no windows, only one small, solid door and an air vent at the top, sticking up out of what looked like a part of the hillside. The cold storage couldn't be found easily, because grass and small shrubs grew on top of it. Only the door and the new porch gave the hideout away. Many years ago the Doukhobors must have dug a huge hole in the hillside, built the cave with these big boulders, and then put the soil back on and around it.

Anneke touched an enormous round rock by the door. It would have taken a group of strong people working together to put the boulders into place, fitting them carefully one on top of the next. The Doukhobors had made the cold storage when several families lived on this hill in big, red-brick houses. The buildings were all gone now. Only some of the foundations, some red bricks, and the cave remained, and some of the old fruit trees farther along the hill.

What would it be like to live in a community, to have so many adults around, and so many kids? Anneke stroked the round rocks. There'd always be others to play with, to help build hideaways. Friends wouldn't have to fib to their parents about whose place they were going to. There'd be adults to look after other adults who needed looking after. There'd be lots of food in the cold storage and probably games and songs and laughter, like she had with Mother on good days. But she'd also have to share her dog and her secret places. Anneke slapped a rock with her flat hand. This was *her* cave and *her* dog, hers alone.

"Get busy," she told herself, grabbing the tool kit Larry and Eileen, her previous foster parents, had given her. Even back then, when she'd turned eight years old, Larry had thought that Anneke was good with tools. He'd given her a real tool kit, not a baby one. Now she took out her tape and measured the diameter of the hole in the ceiling. The pipe would fit perfectly if the top of the air shaft was gone. The chimney had to fit through this opening because there was no other way out.

Armed with her hammer and screwdriver, she climbed up the side of the hill to where the vent stuck out of the earth like a big metal mushroom. Why not use the air shaft as a stovepipe? Would Larry do it that way? Probably.

Going back inside, Anneke jammed the pipe up into the hole. It stayed there, hanging from the ceiling down into the room to almost a metre from the ground. Now all this place needed was a little stove. She'd find one somewhere, the way she'd found the cooler, the old teapot, the cutlery, the dishes, the cooking pot without a handle, and the old kerosene lantern. A little stove would show up, and an axe too.

After searching unsuccessfully for a stove for almost two weeks, Anneke decided the bigger stores in Nelson were the only places to look. So she phoned Larry from the school phone, something she wasn't supposed to do, and asked him out for hamburgers and to go shopping. She'd called her ex-foster parents only a few times over the three years since she'd moved back with Mother. She hiked and camped with them sometimes during the summers. But she always worried a little. Larry and Eileen were too nice, too concerned. They asked too many questions. But now, as always, Larry was delighted to be asked, saying he hadn't seen her for ages.

Anneke didn't tell him what she was looking for and worried about how to get Larry to buy her an old stove and drop it off at the cave without his talking to Mother or seeing the hideout. But once they started browsing around in a second-hand store, the problem was solved. Anneke realized she could *make* a stove just like the one right here in the store. This barrel heater looked a lot like any of the old metal drums that littered the hillside around her trailer. She would find a drum with not too much rust. She also needed to get a special saw to cut a hole for the pipe to fit into.

Pretending to be interested in a square piece of metal with a picture of an apple in the middle, she asked Larry, "How would you cut this?"

"Let's see." He searched along a wall full of tools. "There. A hacksaw. This cuts metal." He held the saw out to her.

By the time they finished looking around the store, she had collected, besides the saw, a water jug, old work gloves, and a bucket. "I'll need some nails and screws too," she said.

"I want to see your projects before I buy you all this," Larry said. "I know it's not very expensive, but . . . I don't know . . ." He studied her closely. "What's up? Why do you suddenly need this?"

Maybe she'd been too greedy, Anneke thought. What if Larry came over to check this out with Mother and found her gone or acting strange? "I don't really *need* any of this stuff," she said casually. "I just thought . . . maybe this summer, well, maybe, uhh . . ." She stalled for time to think before adding, "I want to do more carpentry during the holidays. Everyone else is going somewhere and I'll be bored."

"Hmmm," Larry rubbed his chin. "So do you still use your tool kit?" When Anneke nodded he said, "You always were good with a hammer and saw. How's your mom?"

That was the third time he had asked about Mother. "Oh, fine," she said casually. "She loves to cook, I love to fix things. We have fun. Remember that birdhouse I made when I stayed with you? I do a lot of animal projects now. I carve. And I built Sheera a doghouse."

"OK," Larry said. "I guess your holidays start in two days. We can all go camping. Will you invite us over sometime?"

"Soon." She knew she wouldn't. Besides, she and Mother didn't have a phone.

Two days later Anneke threw her school bag on the heap of coats in the corner of the mudroom. Done! She had finished grade five.

Mother wasn't home again. Anneke frowned. Where could she be this time? Then, shrugging, she took a box of dog biscuits, a box of cookies, three packages of juice mix, a loaf of bread, peanut butter, a new jar of jam, and two apples up to the cooler in her cave. She wanted to get the stove ready and working before Ken came back. He was travelling with his mom and had missed the last two weeks of school. Before he left he had told her he would visit her again at the cave.

After a snack Anneke set to work, banging a crack into the rusty part of an old drum. Next came the difficult job of using the hacksaw to make the opening somewhat round. Even with the work gloves on, her hands hurt by the time she made the hole big enough for the pipe to fit into. Jamming the barrel into place with a few bricks, she said to Sheera, "Come on. Let's eat."

Mother still wasn't home. Anneke looked up and down the street. Mother was starting to wander farther every day, it seemed. I haven't checked her medication either, Anneke thought. I forgot.

She looked for the pills but couldn't find them. After making macaroni and cheese for herself and Sheera, she got her pillow and lay down on the floor to watch TV. She fell asleep, but woke to a loud crash in the kitchen. Sheera didn't bark, so it had to be Mother.

"Ohhhmmm, ohhhmmm," came the chant.

When Anneke blinked through sleepy, half-closed eyes, she saw Mother dressed in heavy snow boots, shorts, and her fake-fur coat. She was holding a smoking twig into a candle flame.

Anneke's eyes flew open. "Put that out. Where were you?"

Mother continued chanting.

Anneke glanced at the clock. "It's after midnight, for heaven's sake." She grabbed the twig and blew out the candle.

Mother still continued chanting.

"I bet you didn't take your medication," Anneke said in exasperation. She felt in her mother's coat pockets, found the pills, and gave her mother one. Then Anneke tucked her into bed and lay down beside her. Soon she heard soft and regular breathing. Quietly, Anneke and Sheera went to their own bedroom.

The next morning when Anneke walked into the kitchen, Mother had already set the table. She turned from the English muffins she was buttering and said, "Good morning. Two poached eggs coming up."

While they ate, Mother asked about school. "Where's your report card?" She used her knife and fork to cut another piece of muffin and egg.

"It's not good," Anneke warned, getting the report from her bag.

Mother scanned the notes. She nodded once or twice, looked up, and said, "It's summer now, but in the fall we'll have to pay more attention to your homework." Then she smiled and added, "You'll be in grade six soon. Let's go to the beach at Slocan River and celebrate with ice cream."

"Sure." Anneke jumped up. "I'll get your beach mat and the sunscreen. Sheera, we'll go for a swim and a long walk." While she packed a swim bag, Anneke hummed happily. Mother was making tuna and pickle sandwiches for a picnic lunch. Like a normal mother. They *were* a normal family, she, Mother, and Sheera.

CHAPTER 2

Anneke's feet felt numb from the cold creek water by the time she finished tying the last twig into place. "Let go," she told Ken, who had been holding his finger on the knot. They clambered up the bank and sat in the sun, warming themselves.

"Good job," she said, as much to herself as to the boy. Yesterday, after Anneke and Mother's outing to the beach, she had run into Ken. He'd shown her his new Japanese book with a picture of a fish trap made of twigs and string. They'd made plans, Ken telling his mom they would build the trap at the library centre, where kids could make things for art camp. Instead, this morning they had hiked to a little lake up above Anneke's place. A steep path, half overgrown, had led them from the cave to a beach. A creek bubbled and rushed down beside the trail, and at the spot where this brook ran out of the lake they'd built the fish trap.

"Let's eat." Ken sat in the sun with his pack.

"What's the lake called?" he asked, his mouth full of ham and mustard sandwich.

"I dunno," Anneke shrugged, biting into her peanut butter sandwich. "Fish Lake," she added, making it up.

"Good name." Ken swatted a fly.

The water was smooth in the heat of the midday sun, but when they first arrived here, early this morning, splashing trout had made rings on the surface of the lake. Anneke planned to come back later tonight, to get the fish that would surely be in the trap by then.

"Did you know my real name is Kenichi?" Ken bit off another mouthful of sandwich before adding, "Ichi means first."

Anneke nodded. "Nice name."

The silence hung suspended between their smiles until she jumped up and asked, "Did you remember to bring your swimming trunks?"

"I'm wearing them." Ken took off his shorts.

Anneke changed behind some thick shrubs, and they swam and chased Sheera in the water. They taught the dog to go to either Ken or Anneke and to bring a stick for one of them to throw.

"This is the smartest breed of dog," Anneke bragged. "Border collies are bred for doing jobs. She's a purebred. Larry and Eileen bought her for me. She was expensive."

"Who are Larry and Eileen?"

"Friends. I stayed at their home for a while way back when I was seven and eight." Anneke swam out from the shore, Sheera following close behind. When they'd almost reached the other side of the small lake, she called, "Come on, the water's warm."

"No way, I can't swim across." Ken stayed close to the beach.

"It's always safe with Sheera around," Anneke yelled. But Ken stayed where he was, so eventually the two swam back to the other shore.

"Don't tell anybody about this place," Anneke told him as they got ready to go home.

He nodded. "Doesn't anyone else ever come here?"

"No, and we'll keep it that way."

"Good." He hoisted his pack over his shoulders. "It'll be our place."

They ran all the way down the hill and yelled their goodbyes. When Anneke walked in the front door of her trailer, she was glad Ken had left.

All the shoes and boots lay nailed to the mudroom floor, big nailheads sticking out of each shoe. Her tool kit stood by the door. Slamming the lid shut, she opened the living room door, prepared for quick action. She froze.

The old carpet was covered with feathers, as if a flock of snow geese had made a crash landing. Empty, cut-up pillow covers and the comforter cover hung like naked bird skins from a chair. In the middle of the room lay a circle made of raw macaroni, and in its centre, like a tiny yellow pyramid, sat the cheese powder.

Angrily Anneke stepped over the mess, feathers

fluttering up with each move she made. "Mother, you're getting worse," she muttered, opening the bedroom door. The room was empty. Mother was gone.

"I'm not cleaning up," Anneke yelled. "I've had enough. I'm going to live by myself in the cave."

Taking the biggest cooking pot from the cupboard, she threw in a stack of newspapers to start the stove's fire, more matches, several boxes of macaroni and cheese, six apples, dog food, a box of cereal, and a bag of powdered milk. She turned to her bedroom, but first went back to the kitchen and added a can of iced tea mix to the pot.

From her bedroom Anneke took the sleeping bag Eileen had made for her eighth birthday. Balancing Sheera's food and water dishes on the top, she carried the load up to the cave. Then she went back for her tool kit. She'd keep that in the cave from now on, too.

When Larry and Eileen had taken her camping, three years ago, they'd all had foam mattresses to sleep on. In the cave the ground was hard. Anneke had no foamy, and she couldn't drag a big and clumsy bed mattress up here either. And now even the pillows were gone. Anneke remembered that a little farther down the valley some farmers had cut hay for their horses. She knew it would be a bit of a walk to get a bagful. "Let's go," she told Sheera.

When she finally got back to the cave with a second garbage bag full of hay, it was starting to get dark. Lying down to test her sleeping spot, her skin prickled, but the softness of the bed made her sigh with pleasure.

Anneke returned to the trailer and took an extra set of clothes, a warm sweater, and two blankets from her bed and piled them up outside the door. From the closet she took a towel, and from the fridge a piece of leftover pizza. Stepping over the feathers again, the tiny yellow pyramid still staring from the centre like an unblinking eye, she closed the door. After two trips to carry all her belongings up the hill, she ate her pizza while Sheera wolfed down some dog food.

With the blankets folded on top of the hay and the towel for a pillow, the bed looked soft and inviting. She crawled into her sleeping bag and closed her eyes. This was home now, a quiet and safe place.

Sheera sighed from her mat. "Come," Anneke said, and the dog was beside her, cuddling against her back for warmth.

Anneke woke, curled up with Sheera like they were two puppies in a warm nest. She wondered what time it was. With the door closed the cave stayed dark, night or day. Ken wouldn't like to sleep here. Then she remembered the new trap. She'd better go right now and bring a fish down to fry for breakfast.

The willow-branch trap held not just one but two trout, flapping around frantically, unable to turn and swim out. Ken would be happy to know that this thing really worked. Maybe she'd go to see him later. With her pocket knife Anneke cut a branch, sharpened the end to a point, and stabbed at the fish, spearing one after several tries. Loosening the trap door at the top, she pulled the still-squirming body out and threw it on the ground. A quick hit with a rock assured her the trout was really dead.

"Sheera, watch the fish," she commanded. "Don't touch." The second trout she flipped back into the lake, saying, "You can live. One is enough."

At the cave Anneke gutted the fish the way Larry had taught her, although it wasn't as easy to slice the belly open with her pocket knife as it had been with his sharp fish knife. She started a small fire in the barrel and put the fish with a little water in the lid from the pot. Carefully she pushed her meal close to the flames.

Carrying the big pot, they walked to where the creek tumbled over some rocks and whirled into a little pool. The pot fit exactly on a flat rock under a tiny waterfall. While the container filled up, Anneke watched a Steller's jay flitting above her from branch to branch. It flew to within a few metres of her, looking for a handout of food, but keeping a sharp eye on Sheera, who was playing with a stick. When the pot was full, the bird flew off with an annoyed screech.

By the time she had lugged the water back to the cave, the fish was cooked. They each ate half, Sheera gobbling hers down in two big bites. After putting the fire out with a little water, Anneke went to find two red bricks. She placed them inside the barrel. If a rack lay on the bricks, the little pot could sit on it, right over the flames. Maybe there was a rack in the kitchen.

At the trailer all was quiet. The shoes still stood motionless, guarding the living room door. The feathers fluttered and danced around the yellow pyramid. Mother must be sleeping, Anneke thought. She walked around carefully, stepping over the feathers and macaroni, until she found what she needed—the rack from the toaster oven. It would fit on the bricks perfectly.

Opening Mother's bedroom door a crack, she looked in. The bed was empty, unmade, but it was never made. Anneke searched the whole trailer. Mother hadn't come back yet. She'd been gone much longer than usual.

Anneke left, determined to let her mother deal with her own mess. As she walked up the hill she wondered if she should go to find Mother. Where *had* Mother spent the night? She was really getting worse. But if Anneke told someone else, they might take Mother away again. I *have* to check her medication more, she decided.

When she reached the top of the field, a car stopped in front of the trailer. Lying down in the tall weeds, Anneke called softly for Sheera to do the same. A man and a woman came out of the car, each carrying a bag. They walked right into the trailer without knocking.

Thieves? Anneke grinned. They could have the

feathers and the macaroni. Sheera gave a soft, low growl. But Anneke shushed her and, followed by her dog, crawled through the waist-high weeds back to the trailer. The windows were always left open in the summer and they headed for the small, high living room window in the back.

From where she crouched, voices but not distinct words floated through to her. Crawling as close as she dared, Anneke heard, ". . . can't go on like this. It's irresponsible." That was the woman's voice.

The man said, "I wonder where her daughter is."

The woman replied, "Maybe she's staying somewhere else. She couldn't be living here, with all this mess."

Anneke grinned. Yes, she was staying somewhere else.

The man said, "The girl went to a foster family a few years ago. Let's see what it says here. Larry and Eileen Proost, down in the valley. Good folks."

The woman said, "I'll collect some things. I wonder if she still uses her medication. Doesn't look like it. Too bad."

A long silence. Anneke wished she'd started checking Mother's medication sooner. From now on she'd keep the pills with her and give Mother one every day. Moving over to her own bedroom window, she peeked in. Nobody was inside. She moved to Mother's room and heard noises—closet door closing, drawer scraping. She didn't look in, for fear of being seen. They were taking some of

Mother's things. Was she back in the hospital? What had she done? Now Anneke wished she'd gone to find Mother last night.

Through the open window she heard the woman calling, "There's another bedroom here, but the bedding is gone. No one slept here last night. I wonder where the daughter is."

"Come," Anneke whispered to Sheera, and they began moving away. Those people wouldn't find her. She'd wait it out in the cave until Mother was well again. The cave was her home.

A short while later the two intruders came outside. They got into the car and drove away. Anneke ran down to the trailer. The shoes, feathers, and macaroni were all in the same places. Mother's pyjamas, housecoat, toothbrush, medication, and some clothes had been taken. Nothing was gone from Anneke's room, but the door stood open. She *always* left it closed.

Locking the front door behind her she said to Sheera, "Nobody gets in here. Mother has her key and I have mine. Let's go home." The dog raced ahead of her up the hill.

Sitting in the sunshine by the entrance, Anneke thought hard. If these people phoned Larry, he'd try to find her. He would think she was lost and in trouble. He didn't know about the cave. Ken knew, but Larry didn't know Ken. Larry would search. He'd get others to search with him. The hillside would be crawling with people. Maybe even dogs. They'd find this place in no time: the porch gave it away. Anneke and Sheera would be like the two fish caught in the trap, unable to get out unseen.

Suddenly in a hurry, she untied the ropes from the trees. The porch wobbled. One firm kick collapsed the structure to one side, and Anneke grabbed her hammer to bang at a post. While separating the wood from the roof board, she scraped her arm on a nail. Tiny droplets of blood appeared. She ignored the cut and worked on until all the posts were removed, the nails pulled out, and the wood stacked along one wall inside the cave. This place could only be used at night, when it was safe. Putting some food, a plastic bag, a rope, her swimsuit, and a towel outside, she locked the door and covered it with dead branches. The chimney easily disappeared under one big branch. Now this hideaway was a hill, just like any other.

With Sheera running ahead of her, Anneke clambered up the trail to Fish Lake. She'd spend the day there and come back tonight to check things out. If everything was safe and undisturbed, she'd try to get in touch with Ken tomorrow and invite him back up to the lake.

Whistling happily, Anneke jumped over some low shrubs and walked into the lake to wash her hands. They were red and sticky from thimbleberry juice. Between swims and whittling pieces of wood into a duck and a squirrel, she'd been eating berries and planning a possible quick escape from the beach.

Throughout the day she'd worked with Sheera on her plan. First they played with a rope, then she taught the dog to pull the rope through the water. Next she tied some small sticks to the end of the rope, as a miniature raft, and showed Sheera how to pull this. By the end of the afternoon they swam across the lake while the dog pulled the tiny raft that held Anneke's clothes in a plastic bag. The clothes stayed dry.

Now Anneke dried herself off. "We'll go home," she said. "The sun is gone and it'll start getting dark soon."

Sheera wagged her tail.

"Yes, you're tired too. Time for supper and bed. I'll make—"

Sheera growled. She stood up on her hind legs, sniffed furiously, and came down on all four legs, facing the thimbleberry bushes.

"What is it, girl?"

The dog gave a deep growl, then started barking, her tail down, ears back, the fur on her neck raised. She stood tense as a spring, but didn't go toward the bush. All her signals meant *danger*.

In a hurry, Anneke finished buttoning up her shorts and pulled her T-shirt over her head. While struggling to get one arm into the sleeve, she saw it: two eyes, yellow eyes, big yellow cat eyes, glaring.

The head moved forward, ever so slightly. Sheera barked wildly and moved closer to Anneke, standing in front of her.

Cougar! One of the West Kootenays' most

dangerous animals. Bear, play dead and dumb; cat, play big and brave. Stare back. Anneke puffed out her chest and broadened her shoulders. She spread her arms up and out. "Ahrrrrr," she yelled, loudly, angrily. Sheera barked. Anneke yelled. The hard eyes stared, unblinking. The head moved forward. Anneke saw the front legs, powerful and ready to jump. It was as if the animal were standing still, yet coming forward. Closer. Closer.

Anneke noticed, just to the left of her, the thick, heavy stick they'd been playing with earlier. She moved ever so slightly and felt Sheera's rump bang into her legs. The dog barked, snarled, growled at the cougar. Yelling fiercely, Anneke moved like a flash. She grabbed the stick and swung it, whipping the weapon above her head with both arms.

Cougars kill. Keep eye contact.

Still the wildcat came closer. Closer. Too close.

Sheera backed farther into Anneke's legs. The cougar lunged forward. Almost at the same time Anneke smacked the stick down on the cat's head. Crack!

The cougar lunged at Sheera. Teeth snapped, bit, ripped. Snarls of anger. Yelps of pain. Teeth tore at fur, at flesh. Blood flowed.

Anneke's head pounded with fear. She cracked the stick again. Again. Again. *Fight. Fight for your dog.* Arm muscles strained, screaming with effort, with fear. Crack. Full across the yellow eyes.

A roar. The cougar fled. Twigs cracked. Anneke still clutched one end of the broken stick.

She sank down on her knees beside her dog, breath screaming from her lungs. Sheera whined. Blood ran from the dog's face, her ear, her leg. Red streaks ran onto her paw and dripped onto the ground.

Anneke stroked her pet. "You're brave," she said, her voice shaky and hoarse from the yelling. "You saved my life. And I saved yours. We're a team."

They backed up to the water, their hearts still pounding, their eyes on the bushes. Washing her dog gently, Anneke cleaned the blood and inspected the cuts. A little piece of flesh was torn from one ear. It would heal. The dog's nose showed a small gash. But the chest had a deep cut that ran down to the leg, where cougar bites bled heavily. After washing the wounds, Anneke moved Sheera's leg. The dog whimpered a little, but the movements seemed fine. That meant she didn't have any broken bones.

Anneke took off her T-shirt and tried to wind it around her dog's leg, but the cloth was too thick. Still keeping her eyes on the bushes and her ears tuned for noises, she took her knife from her key ring, cut a sleeve from her shirt, tore it into two strips and wound them around the injured leg. She did the same with her other sleeve.

"Let's go home," she whispered, hugging and petting her dog. They moved down the hill slowly, Sheera limping.

The cave was undisturbed. Anneke removed the branches, unlocked the door, made a fire, and put water on the rack inside the barrel. Macaroni and cheese would be a good meal to share right now.

The bandages were soaked through with blood. Gently she unwrapped them and rinsed them out. Sheera settled on her mat to lick her leg. The bleeding stopped. After lighting a candle, Anneke closed the door. The day was over. They hadn't been found.

CHAPTER 3

In the morning Sheera's wounds looked a bit better. Thin scabs had formed on her ear and nose. The teeth marks on her leg still looked sore. Anneke wanted to wrap the leg up again, to keep it clean. But Sheera decided otherwise, pulling the cloth off and licking the wounds. She didn't limp quite as much as yesterday.

Anneke fed her dog and ate some bread with jam and peanut butter. She wanted to go back up to the lake, in case Larry came looking for her. She didn't feel safe around the trailer or the cave during the day. She didn't feel safe looking for Ken either. But was it safe up at the lake? Anneke decided she and Sheera would have to check things out.

Armed with a heavy stick, her bathing suit, and food for the day, they set off on the trail. Sheera hesitated at the first bend, sitting back and sniffing the air. Anneke's body tensed. She took one step forward. Another. No sign of cougar. Sheera walked behind her now, sniffing furiously, nervously. Anneke sat down on the trail to calm her banging heart. She hugged her pet. "What do you smell?" she asked. The dog's ears stood up a little more, but otherwise nothing moved. After a short rest the two walked on, slowly, silently, as if stalking the cougar that had stalked them.

They reached the lake without noticing anything unusual. The beach lay still in the sunlight, the fish trap empty and undisturbed. There were no sounds except for the occasional splash of a fish in the water.

Sheera smelled the bushes carefully for a long time, Anneke standing behind her with the big stick, ready to strike. Finally the dog settled down to lick her chest and leg.

Anneke sighed with relief. She sat against her favourite tree with a piece of wood, turning it over and over in her hands, studying the shape from all sides. If she cut a chunk off the top, this might become a swimming duck. Taking her knife from her belt, she started carving. From time to time she stopped to scan the bushes with her eyes or to go for a swim. Sheera was always ready to follow her into the water for a swim across the lake. The dog had calmed down and no longer seemed as nervous as she had in the early morning, although she frequently smelled the air and checked every sound. Anneke kept her big stick handy, just in case.

As the hot afternoon drew to a close, they still hadn't noticed any signs of wildlife. The only animals around, besides Sheera and the fish that had started jumping again, were a wooden duck and a dog that Anneke had carved.

Larry had been right when he said she had talent and might be a carver one day, or a carpenter. She felt grateful for his trust and for this knife he'd given her. But what was Larry up to now? Was he looking for her? There had been no noises of people searching the hillside.

Anneke considered her options. She could come up here every day until people forgot about her. She could go to Larry's, or ask Ken up here. She could go into the trailer and look for money for food. Mother probably wouldn't be back for a few days. That man and woman who had come to the trailer would help her to get counselling and perhaps better medication.

Anneke felt bored. No, not exactly bored, but restless, unsure. Were people actually searching for her? And what *had* happened to Mother?

"Enough of this waiting," she said. "Let's go. We'll investigate." Sheera wagged her tail in response.

The cave's door sat locked behind the branches. Anneke approached the trailer cautiously, but she saw nothing out of place. When she peeked in, she noticed that Mother's strange feathered message still covered the living room floor.

Night was falling. Anneke and Sheera used the cover of semi-darkness to run down the street and check at Ken's house. The curtains were closed. His mom's car sat in the driveway. Anneke didn't want to ring the bell. She decided to walk to Larry and Eileen's place in the valley and look in the windows. She knew they never closed their curtains in the summer. Anneke would be able to see if the adults were watching television or reading, unworried. Their daughter, Elishia, was likely in bed by now. Perhaps Larry was off, searching.

By the time they arrived at the house in the country, over an hour's walk, Sheera was limping more again. The stars and a small slice of moon accented the vastness above. Walking down the long driveway, avoiding potholes, Anneke saw she'd arrived too late. The lights were out, the house asleep. Tired from the long walk, she sat on the garden bench. Sheera lay down on her feet. They stayed there for quite a while, the outside air feeling a lot warmer than the temperature in the cave. Anneke decided to cuddle up with her pet and stay here for the night.

They found a space under an old apple tree at the edge of the lawn, protected, yet close enough to the front windows. From here they'd notice if any action went on in the house. Sheera groaned, lay down, and licked her leg.

Some time later, Anneke woke to the sound of a car coming up the driveway. Whispering to her dog to be still, they backed up farther under the tree. The car's doors closed. A few minutes later the house lights came on.

Through the window Anneke saw Eileen holding Elishia in her arms. Larry put his hands on his wife's shoulders and kissed her forehead. Then he bent and kissed his daughter before Eileen carried her off to bed.

Anneke's gaze stayed on the lighted space where the family had stood. Had Eileen carried her that way when she lived here as their foster child? Had the adults kissed her sleeping face? No, Elishia was only three. Anneke had been seven and eight back then. Too big to be carried. Besides, she wasn't their own child. Had Mother ever carried her like that? No, Mother didn't carry. Mother wasn't strong.

Elishia's bedroom window turned dark. That room was not the one where Anneke used to sleep. Larry had told her several times that her room was still there if she ever needed it again. She could go in now and crawl into the bed, with Sheera sleeping on the mat, the way it was back then.

She closed her eyes and imagined how she'd be babied, fussed over, maybe even kissed goodnight. Larry would ask her a million questions about herself, about Mother. She could almost hear his voice now. "But how are you *really* doing, Anneke?"

"Fine," she'd say. But he'd ask again, stressing the word "really" even more, as if she weren't telling the truth.

Things *were* fine. The two of them managed very well on their own. Hadn't they just beaten back a cougar yesterday? Hadn't she made them a comfortable home in the cave?

Anneke's eyes came back to where she'd watched the three people in the living room. The lighted window beamed out in the darkness like a beacon. Anneke almost—almost—got up to go inside.

Then Larry walked in front of the window with the phone. Nodding his head, he listened. Eileen came up and stood beside him. She looked tired and sad. He put the phone down. The light switched off. The bedroom and bathroom lights were on for a short time before the household went to sleep.

The moon had moved slightly in the blackness above. Anneke put her head on Sheera's warm belly and closed her eyes.

She woke when a car door slammed. A soft morning drizzle fell, but the apple tree, like a giant umbrella, kept out the misty rain. It must have sprinkled for a while, though, because big drops had gathered on the leaves. They plopped down everywhere.

Sheera yawned and did her wake-up stretch: first her two front legs, all the way out, bum in the air, then her two back legs. Next came a good shake from nose to tail tip and the dog was ready for her day. She almost didn't limp this morning. Anneke wished, not for the first time, that she herself was a dog. Shivering in her wet, sleeveless T-shirt, she stretched and shook too, but didn't feel any better at all.

The car drove off. Anneke jumped up, rushed to the driveway, and saw two heads in the vehicle just before it drove out of sight. Good. The house was empty. She could go inside and get dry.

The door was locked, of course. Larry always locked things. It was in this house that Anneke had first learned to use an electric drill to screw a latch onto a door frame. Checking the windows, she found only the bathroom window open. It was too high.

Sheera whimpered. She must be hungry. They hadn't eaten since yesterday when, at Fish Lake, they'd both had bread and jam for lunch. Anneke's stomach felt like a huge hole in the middle of her body. Dragging a tall block of firewood underneath the bathroom window, she told Sheera they'd just go in to dry off and get something to eat. From this higher position Anneke managed to slide the screen across and off the window, then hoist herself up and into the opening. She lay there for a minute with her stomach on the windowsill before sliding, hands first, down to the back of the toilet. From there she slid to the toilet seat and finally to the bathroom floor. For once it was nice to be so scrawny.

Taking off her shoes and all her clothes, she grabbed Larry's bathrobe, which hung on the door, and hurried around to the back. She let Sheera in and put her clothes and shoes in the dryer. The fridge held orange juice, yogurt, pudding, sliced meat, bread, milk, eggs. First they shared the pudding. Then Anneke made egg-in-a-nest for herself. While she ate the fried slices of bread with eggs in the middle and drank orange juice, Sheera feasted on pieces of bread soaked in milk and egg. What a meal! Anneke patted her stomach, now a balloon instead of a hole, and burped loudly.

With her clothes still drying, she washed the dishes and cleaned the muddy spots in the bathroom. Then she wandered upstairs to her old room. A large, framed photo of her with Larry and Eileen hiking at Valhalla Park stood on the dresser. She ran her hand over the flowered bedspread, the pillow, the nightstand with a picture of her holding Sheera, then a cute, fluffy puppy, in her arms. They had lived here when Sheera first learned to sit, to fetch, to play ball. Of course Anneke was only a little kid then, with longer hair. These days she sported a short cut. But the blue eyes that smiled from the picture's thin face were the same ones that now looked back at her from the mirror above the dresser. Except today her eyes were not smiling.

She left the room, closing the door with a bang, and peeked into Elishia's bedroom, just to see what the space of a real daughter looked like. The stuffed animals, matching curtains and bedspread decorated with colourful clowns, the shelf full of books and toys made her walk farther into the room. The bed felt soft, cozy. Back then Larry or Eileen had read Anneke a story every night. She had owned a teddy bear called Pooch and a bunny named Fluffers when this was her home. Those stuffed animals had long since disappeared. Briefly her mind flashed on the picture of the family standing in the lighted room last night—together, holding each other. Grabbing a bunny from the shelf, Anneke tucked the small pink animal inside the bathrobe and left the room. On a step she sat down and took out the toy. It was so different from how Fluffers had felt back then. Her own bunny had been bigger, much fluffier, with longer ears and a happier face. Fluffers had been so soft, so safe to hold at night. But everything was different now. She didn't live here anymore—now she was breaking in.

Sheera put her head on Anneke's knee and looked at the bunny. "No, you can't have it," she said, hugging her dog. "I can't, either. This place isn't our home." She put the bunny back and dressed in her warm, dry clothes. Just for a moment she considered phoning Ken from here. But it was too risky.

They left through the back door. Replacing the bathroom window screen was no easy task, but finally the frame slid into the groove. Anneke put the piece of firewood back in the shed and followed Sheera down the road, in the direction of her cave.

Approaching the trailer cautiously from the back, Anneke stayed low in the tall grass, holding Sheera with one hand. When nothing moved, she ran up to the door, knocked loudly, and hid again. No one came. Instructing Sheera to stay and watch, Anneke quickly took the key from her belt ring, unlocked the door, and peeked in. The mudroom had never looked so organized, with coats hanging on hooks and shoes standing in pairs under them. She checked one of her shoes. Yes, there was a hole left by a nail.

The living room also looked clean, the feathers and macaroni gone. The doors to the bedrooms stood wide open. Anneke closed hers, wishing she had a spare padlock. Checking out her mother's closet, she noticed that most of the clothes were gone. So Mother was being looked after somewhere. Anneke wondered how long the mental breakdown would last this time. Hopefully only a few weeks, at most until the end of summer.

The fridge stood empty, although the freezer section held one can of frozen orange juice. In the cupboard Anneke found dog food, biscuits, cereal, juice mix, crackers, and even some dried fruit bars. She put everything in two plastic bags and carried them up the hill. In the cave she packed a lunch and left the rest of the food in the cooler. After locking up, she hid the cave door behind branches and hiked to Fish Lake.

Sheera sniffed furiously as they walked up the path. At every bend Anneke stopped and listened for animal sounds, looked for signs of cougar paws on the trail. No wildlife showed. No twigs snapped. Nothing moved.

As soon as they reached the day camp she saw the fish trap. Something strong had ripped the top off. Parts of string and broken twigs lay scattered. Then, the sign: a bear paw mark in the wet sand. Anneke put her fist on the print the way Larry had taught her. Her knuckles barely fit, so the animal was small. But still, a bear! Sheera sniffed the sand. She growled a deep, throaty growl.

"We'll have to be careful and make lots of noise," Anneke said loudly. Larry had taught her to let a bear know when you were around, so the animal would probably leave the area.

"Let's look," she called into the morning stillness. "Come on, Sheera, we'll be noisy today."

The bear must have taken a fish from the trap and left. Anneke found no further signs. Sheera stopped sniffing and lay down at the water's edge, but her eyes never left the growth along the beach and her ears stayed up.

"I'll teach you how to sing," Anneke grinned. "We'll sing together and scare everything away. Owww, ow, ow, owwwww," she called, throwing her head back.

Sheera ran over and barked, tail wagging. They romped on the sand for a while before Anneke looked at the fish trap closely again. Tomorrow she'd bring some string for repairs. Taking out her knife and a chunk of wood, she joined her dog in the shade. The day would be hot and long.

"I'll tell you about when you were little." Anneke needed to hear her own voice as a warning to the bear. "Once upon a time there was this fluffy little black and white puppy with the most amazing brown eyes."

Sheera pricked up her ears. A soft growl rumbled from deep inside her throat. Anneke jumped up, her heart pounding. She'd heard a noise too. A twig cracking. Steps coming from the partly overgrown path. Careful, slow steps. The bear? The cougar? People looking for her? Whoever it was, she'd have to outsmart it. Bear, play dead and dumb; cat, play big and brave; adults—how to play adults?

"Come." Running over and crouching behind a nearby thimbleberry bush, she motioned for Sheera to be still.

On the beach lay her knife and the chunk of wood, the lunch, her bathing suit, and her shoes: a dead giveaway. So much for outsmarting, she scoffed.

Something moved at the trail end. Ken!

Anneke jumped up. "I thought you were the bear."

"The bear?" Ken's eyes got big. He dropped his pack and looked around anxiously. "Where?"

"The trap is wrecked." She pointed to the broken branches.

"Where is it?" Ken walked backwards from the trap, his eyes scanning the forest.

"Gone." Happy and relieved to see her friend, Anneke showed him the damage and the paw mark.

"Gee, I sure wouldn't want to meet a bear

coming up here." Ken moved his pack to an open stretch of beach away from the trailhead and the bushes. He wiped his face with his T-shirt and sighed. "Phew. It's hot already." Rummaging in his pack, he found two apples, holding one out to her. "I figured you'd be up here somewhere, but I didn't know if I'd find you. I can't stay long." He looked around nervously.

Anneke took a big bite of apple, needing to fill her mouth to stop herself from babbling. She wanted to talk, talk about everything. But caution stopped her. First Ken had better tell her why he was here.

"You're in the paper. They're looking for you." He pulled a newspaper from his pack and opened it.

Anneke stared at a picture of her at the fall fair at age eight, holding the wooden dog she'd carved back then while staying at Larry and Eileen's. "That's . . ." she mumbled, looking up at Ken. "How did they . . ."

"Read it." He pointed to the headline.

"Young artist eludes searchers," Anneke read out loud. She didn't know what "eludes" meant and wouldn't ask. Slowly, stumbling a little over a few of the bigger words, she read silently that Mother was in the hospital after being hit by a car.

Anneke bit her lip, wishing she'd tried harder to find Mother that night. Her hands crumpled the edges of the newspaper. She needed to hold something tightly, and, even though she was sitting, she felt as if she were falling. Mother was hurt. "How's she doing?" she whispered.

"On the news on TV they said she's fine."

"TV? Oh." The article said that on the second day Mother had asked about her daughter, Anneke, only the newspaper spelled her name Annekke. It also said that since no one knew of the daughter's whereabouts, the police were organizing a search of the whole valley. To her horror the paper talked about how Larry had found the cave with her belongings in it.

The reporter quoted Larry as saying, "She's clever and knows how to look after herself. It'll be hard to find her if she doesn't want to be found. I think she just needs some space and she'll come out on her own."

The story went on to talk about Larry being her foster father once and about Mother's mental illness. Anneke blushed. She didn't want to look at Ken, felt his eyes on her.

Finally, forcing herself to look straight at him, she said defiantly, "What do *they* know!" Crumpling the paper, she threw it on the ground.

Ken shrugged. "I thought you'd want to read it."

"Sure. He thinks he still needs to look after me."

Ken put the paper back in his pack. "Do you have a real dad?" he asked.

"No." Anneke flicked an ant off her leg.

"I don't either. Well, I do, of course. But my mom's divorced."

"My mother says she doesn't remember anything

about my father. I'm never ever allowed to talk about him and I've never met him. My mother is . . ." Anneke left the words hanging in the stillness over the lake.

Ken unpacked a bag of food: another apple, two oranges, cookies, and a rice ball wrapped in strips of green stuff.

Anneke held the big, round ball up and looked at it questioningly.

"Japanese," her friend said. "That's nori, seaweed. Sorry, there was no bread. This is all I could take. I didn't want Mom to notice."

She nodded. He hadn't talked to others about her.

Ken said, "This guy, Larry, and a woman and a little kid were at your trailer last night, cleaning up and waiting for you."

Anneke grinned. So Larry and Eileen had worked at her place while she was at their house under the apple tree.

"Do you want me to come back?" he asked, getting up and scanning the thick woods again. "I'll be missed if I don't get home soon. Mom's making barbecued chicken for the searchers. I could try to bring you some."

Anneke shrugged. Barbecued chicken. That was Larry and Eileen's favourite food. "Thanks, but I don't know if I'll be here tomorrow. Thanks for the food, though."

"I can't believe you're hiding like this. I wouldn't have the nerve." He looked around, then at her, a look of admiration in his eyes. "I only stay at home and read about stuff like this. You're actually doing it."

She looked at him, wishing she could just stay at home too. Wishing Mother were in the trailer right now. She said nothing but nodded when he got up and repeated that he'd better get back.

The whole hillside would be crawling with people. "Come on, Sheera, let's hurry. We're not going back to the cave." She put her food, clothes, and carved animals in a plastic bag, then tied it to the little raft. The fish trap was too valuable to destroy completely, so some branches thrown over the structure would have to do for cover. With another branch she swept the ground clean of any visible traces of foot and paw prints.

Satisfied with her work, Anneke stepped into the lake, gave the raft rope to Sheera to pull, and set off for the opposite shore. Let the people search, even with dogs. She knew how to stay hidden, to keep the searchers from finding them, or even their scent.

At the other end of Fish Lake they walked up the stream for quite a while. Finally they stopped by a huge tree trunk where yesterday she had stashed some small, woven mats under a root.

Now came the hard part. Anneke was grateful for the tricks a Native teacher had taught them in grade four. "Remember, Sheera, we practised this yesterday. Be good." The dog sat down in the creek and hesitantly held up one leg. A little mat of woven sticks and weeds fitted around the paw. Anneke tied grass socks around all four paws and under her own feet as well. "You're good," she told her dog, who looked miserable. Sheera hated walking while tied into the little mats. But they needed to get up and away from the bank along the creek without leaving a scent.

Carefully Anneke swept away any tracks they made with a branch as they moved slowly into the forest. There she untied the grass socks and stashed them under a bush. Shrugging out of her wet bathing suit, she untied the plastic bag with her dry clothes from the raft. While the search went on down below they'd be up here with food, water, and lots of wood to whittle.

CHAPTER 4

All afternoon Anneke had enjoyed romping with Sheera, chasing her dog around the big trees, playing hide and seek, whittling a piece of wood into a fish, and making a bed of leaves and pine needles for the two of them. Not once had they seen large animals or heard any sounds of searchers coming up the creek. Now, as darkness set in, she lay down to try out the bed. It felt prickly, hard, and uncomfortable, not at all like her cozy nest in the cave. She wore only her T-shirt and shorts. How stupid not to have brought anything else. Larry had taught her to be prepared for sudden weather changes in the mountains. "Always bring your sweater and rain gear, even on a hot and sunny day," he used to tell her.

She'd forgotten. The last time she had camped with Larry and Eileen, Elishia had been only two years old. Anneke wondered if Larry was teaching the little girl things about nature yet, about fishing, about fire safety, how to cook food on an open fire. Next time she saw Larry, maybe she . . . Anneke scowled. If she saw Larry, she'd be caught. "No way," she mumbled, sitting up from the prickly bed and scratching her arms.

She'd stay out here in the mountains for a long time, until Mother came home. How was Mother doing, anyway? Was the doctor keeping her in the hospital for new medication or because of the accident? Anneke wished she'd set up a system with Ken, a place for him to drop off notes. And food too. She and Sheera had eaten all their other food today—they had none left.

Imagine that, news about her was in the paper. On TV even. While rubbing her cold legs, Anneke wondered if the reporters showed the cave on the news. No, not the cave. That was hers and hers alone.

Suddenly, surprised out of her thoughts, she looked up. Was that a flashlight? Sheera crept closer and settled against the front of Anneke's body, her head on the girl's lap.

Again a light flashed from somewhere through the trees. From above the trees. Had searchers found them *here*, in the dark, in the forest? Then came a long, slow, deep rumble that rolled and echoed around them like a sonic avalanche. Thunder! Sheera whimpered and pushed even closer against Anneke.

"Be brave," she said, as much to herself as to Sheera, hugging her pet close. Another flash of lightning lit up the sky, momentarily illuminating the swaying treetops as clearly as if it were daylight. The wind picked up. Branches swished and rustled. Thunder clapped so close overhead, so deafeningly, it made both of them jump. Anneke grabbed the dog's head and held it tightly.

Rain began. Large drops fell between trees, first only a few, then more, more, until they could not escape the torrent of water streaming down on them, the thick branches no longer providing shelter.

She clutched her dog around the neck. They lay on the ground, soaked, shaking. With each booming thunderclap Sheera whimpered, her head pushing harder against Anneke's body. Even though her eyes were closed, Anneke could tell when lightning flashed.

The wind still whipped the trees. A branch snapped and crashed to the ground. Sheera gave a sharp whine. "Shhh, shhh, be brave," Anneke whispered, her voice trembling.

Rain pounded down, sounding like one relentless drum roll. Trees creaked, moaned. Thunder cracked, echoed, rolled on and on down through the valley.

Slowly the storm moved off, to pummel the next mountaintop. Anneke loosened her fingers, stiff from gripping Sheera's fur so tightly. "We're OK, puppy," she whispered, stroking the trembling head. "You're a good dog."

From time to time lightning still brightened the

sky, but the thunder became more distant, now coming several seconds after the lightning. The rain did not let up, though. Larry would be happy with all this water. "Less chance of a forest fire," he used to explain. Easy for him to say. He was dry, in his soft bed, under blankets. Maybe he even closed the windows. No, not Larry. He liked fresh air.

The pine needles prickled Anneke's bare skin. She shivered as huge drops of rain fell on her. Hugging Sheera didn't give any warmth because the dog's long hair was soaked right through. Complete darkness had settled in among the trees and when Anneke looked around her, she could not even see the dark shapes of trees any longer. A rain drop hit her eye. Angrily, determined not to cry, she wiped it away.

Leaning back against a tree trunk, she listened as water fell from the branches. Was rain actually still coming from the sky, or were the trees just shedding their wet load? Why not go back to the lake? At least it wouldn't be so dark out there under the open sky.

"Let's go," she told Sheera. Crawling on her hands and knees on the wet ground, Anneke searched for her bundle of belongings. Needles stuck to her hands and bare arms. "Ouch!" she cried when her knee pressed down hard on a prickly cone.

No bundle. "Think," she told herself. "Where did I put it? The tree is behind me, this big root I feel is on my left. It has to be close." Her hands kept searching, feeling muck, cones, sharp bits of sticks, and finally the bundle.

She took her belongings, stood up, straightened, screamed. She dropped the bundle, flailing her arms around her head. She slapped at a wet thing, a cold, slimy object that stuck to her face. She screamed again and smacked at the clutching wrap, trying to get the gluey cover away from her face, but the sopping shroud clung to her hair, her forehead, her eyes.

Sheera, her nose pushed against Anneke's stomach, gave a questioning bark.

Eventually Anneke stopped swinging her arms, stopped flapping at the object. She realized it was her wet bathing suit, hanging from a branch just above her head.

"I'm losing my cool," she mumbled, feeling stupid. After yanking the bathing suit down and finding her other belongings again, she sat against the tree for a minute to think.

Big drops of rain continued to fall. Searchers wouldn't be coming up here tonight. She could safely go back to the beach and stay there. Everything was soaked anyway. She might as well swim back across the lake, wash this itchy muck off her arms and legs, and see if the rain had stopped. At least the sand was softer to sleep on than these needles.

Standing up, she started to move forward, then stopped. Which way to the creek? Usually from here the rushing water gave her direction. But now

Anneke heard only the sounds of big drops splattering as they hit the ground. She listened intently. No creek.

They'd have to wait—but this rain might keep dripping all night. Defeated, she sat down again, feeling tired, very tired. Her body was crying to lie down flat. Finding the soggy bed of needles and leaves, Anneke curled up on it. Sheera lay down beside her. Hugging her pet, she murmured, "What a mess." The dog sighed in answer.

Something woke them. Sheera sat up and growled. Anneke tensed, waiting and listening in the blackness until she felt the animal relaxing in her arms. Maybe the movement of a small animal had spooked the dog. A few leftover drops splattered to the ground like notes that accompanied the quiet background music of the stream strumming and playing over the rocks.

"The creek!" Anneke shouted. She grabbed her belongings and they made their way cautiously through the dark forest, Sheera leading, knowing exactly where they were going. As the rushing of water became louder, Anneke saw lightness through the thinning branches. The half moon and stars brightened the open sky above. Kneeling, she let the water wash her arms and legs clean.

Still shaking from the cold, her teeth now chattering, she walked in her wet clothes down the creek and swam across the lake. They rested on the beach, dripping, shivering, but feeling much safer.

"We'll get the sleeping bag and the cooler from the cave," she told Sheera. "We need them. People will look for me, probably early in the morning, as soon as it's light. I can make a tiny fire in the stove to warm us up before we go deeper into the forest."

Carefully they slipped and slithered down the steep, wet path. Here and there the small creek had overflowed its banks and Anneke walked ankle deep in rushing water. As they came to the edge of the forest, she froze. A light shone from the trailer's living room window. A figure moved around inside.

Mother! Anneke's heart skipped for joy. She could go in, get dry, be warm, stay home again. Things were back to normal.

Running down the hill, she stopped suddenly. The figure in the window turned. It wasn't Mother. It was Eileen. Anneke saw the woman clearly before she moved away from the window. The light switched off.

Why was Eileen in the trailer? Where was Larry? They'd come to get her. Anneke stood motionless for a few minutes, hardly breathing, before she moved back towards the cave, careful not to make any noises. She had to get her stuff out of there. Now. *Fast!*

The door to the cave stood ajar, with no branches, no lock. Motioning for Sheera to stay and wait, Anneke crept toward the door, ever so slowly. She heard a soft snoring. Larry snored. Nothing was visible inside the dark cave, but that had to be him.

Then she saw his shoes sitting at the cave entrance. Cautiously she moved back to her dog, thinking, Larry is here. Eileen is in the trailer. Then Elishia must be there too, probably sleeping in Anneke's bed. And Eileen in Mother's bed. How dare they! Had they picked the lock or crawled in the bathroom window? She had to grin at that thought.

Then another thought pushed its way into her tired brain. If they were here, then their house was empty. Anneke felt hungry and cold—especially cold. "Sheera, come," she whispered. "We have a warm house to sleep in. A bed. And a fridge full of food."

As they hurried down the lamp-lit stretch of road, Anneke saw a bicycle in Ken's neighbour's yard. She'd borrow it, just for the night, and leave a note asking Larry to return the bike tomorrow.

Riding onto the darker valley road, her body felt less stiff and cold. She called happily to her dog, "Food, Sheera, and a bed. Blankets. A *real* pillow. Let's go." Faster she rode, faster, to Larry's driveway.

Approaching the house, Anneke slowed down. She hid the bicycle in the bushes along the driveway and told Sheera to stay. Walking quietly to the front door she knocked loudly, hid, and waited. No one came. Ringing the bell also brought no response. The door was locked, the house empty.

Getting in through the bathroom window was easy. She peeled off her wet clothes and left them where they fell. Finding a large, long-sleeved shirt in Eileen's drawer, she slipped it on. The fridge offered leftover chocolate cake as well as ham, peas, and strawberries. She ate all the cake first while the dog gobbled down the ham in huge bites. Anneke finished the peas. The strawberries they shared.

Up in her old room, Anneke crawled into bed. Sheera circled on her mat a few times and flopped down. The clock showed 4:12 a.m.

The clock radio in the next room came on, and Anneke heard someone talking about some kind of problem with flooded fields. She looked at her clock: 6:56 a.m. Groaning, she turned over and hid her head under the pillow. The now-muffled voice droned on.

Almost tripping over Sheera, who lay curled up beside the bed, Anneke stumbled across the room and walked into the door post. "Ouch!" Why did Larry always leave his radio turned up so *loudly?* Groggily she shuffled to the other bedroom, rubbed her bleary eyes, and tried unsuccessfully to focus on all the buttons. While she leaned closer, the seven o'clock news came on.

"Today's headlines: an earthquake rocks central Asia, and a local girl is still lost in the mountains."

Anneke hesitated, listening.

"Eleven-year-old Anneke Droste, missing since Monday, is thought to have spent the night in the forest during a thunderstorm. Her foster father, Larry . . ."

Anneke scowled. He was *not* her foster father anymore.

". . . to the girl's hideaway above the trailer last night, but he found it empty. Food and a sleeping bag were left in the hideaway. Police speculate the girl planned to return last night, but met with difficulties."

Anneke grimaced. Yes, difficulties. People who wouldn't leave her alone.

"A massive search of Lustre Lake, Dusty Creek, and the surrounding forest is currently underway. So far there has been no sign of the girl. In other news, central—"

Anneke pushed several buttons on the top of the radio until the noise stopped. She chuckled. A massive search. Good. That meant they'd all be busy over there, so she could stay here for the day. No danger of being found in this house. Lustre Lake. Humph. Better tell Ken sometime what they really called Fish Lake. Sheera's nose pushed at her hand questioningly.

"Do your thing," Anneke yawned, taking the dog to the front yard. Leaning against the door, waiting, she knew she'd sleep for most of the day.

In the middle of the afternoon they woke up. Anneke let Sheera out, put her damp clothes in the dryer, and took a shower. She made mushroom soup from a can, pouring half of it over some pieces of bread in a dish for Sheera. Next came a cheese and mayo sandwich for herself, then a fried egg for each of them. Too bad she had already eaten the chocolate cake and the strawberries.

They wandered out into the afternoon heat. The last of the thunderclouds had completely disappeared. From the deck the view of the mountains spread out past the sandbox, the lawn, the fruit trees, and the tall hedges that ringed the property like the walls around a castle.

The garden looked lush and green. There, in the heat of the summer, grew small carrots. And lots of yummy bright red currants. Sheera spotted a few ripe strawberries and Anneke gathered fresh green peas. Taking everything inside, they sat together on the living room floor, sharing their finds, Sheera already drooling before she tasted her first red currant.

Life at Larry and Eileen's was so different from her own life, either at the trailer or in the woods. If she ever decided to stay here there'd be lots of food all the time. And no wild animals, or nights in the rain under a dripping tree. No worries. Would anyone come to this house today and find her here? What would she do if someone arrived? Hide? Be found and live here?

"I won't think about that right now," she told Sheera. "Let's watch the news and see if the lost girl has been found yet." She chuckled. Maybe a reporter would show the trailer with Eileen and Elishia on TV. Or Larry. Maybe the trailer was used as their search-and-rescue headquarters. Anneke wished they hadn't found the cave.

Curled up on the couch with a soft drink, Sheera beside her, she switched back and forth between the only two channels Larry and Eileen could get with their antenna. Neither program showed any news. How annoying. When she turned to the news on the radio, the announcer mentioned only that search dogs had sniffed out an overnight camp in the forest, presumed to have been used by the girl and her dog. They had not yet been located, the announcer said. Search-and-rescue members were increasing their efforts to find them before nightfall.

Later, the TV news ran an interview with Larry. His eyes had big black circles under them and stubble grew on his chin. He said how sorry he was not to have checked on her sooner. How he hoped she was safe somewhere.

Anneke wanted to say, *Don't worry, Larry, I'm OK.*

Eileen stood in the background, facing away from the camera, talking to an older woman. Then she leaned her head on the other woman's shoulder. Was that Eileen's mother? Anneke felt sorry for Eileen, but then she thought about her own mother. Of course she wasn't there. The news said nothing about her, as if Mother didn't exist. Anneke's throat felt funny, thick and full. She cleared it and rubbed her eyes. Crying wouldn't help.

"Come on, dog," she said. "We'll play fetch." They went out into the late-afternoon air.

Later they ate again and watched TV for a few hours, sitcoms only. There was no news on either of the two channels. Bored, Anneke looked through Elishia's room for something to do. Finding nothing, she searched Eileen's hobby room and found a sewing machine, ironing board, cutting table. Eileen must be mostly sewing these days. She used to sketch a lot, but no paper and pencils lay around anywhere now. On the table lay a half-finished dress for Elishia.

Eileen had made a pair of pants and a shirt for Anneke when she lived here. Mother used to sew too, before she got sick. Anneke remembered, when she was a really small girl, being all excited to see pieces of material grow into something that fit her exactly. Mother had even made her a cloth doll for her fourth birthday. That was when Mother still called her Kindeke, which meant "little child" in Dutch. "My Kindeke," she used to say as she hugged Anneke to her, or carried her on her bony hip. And Anneke called her Mama, and combed her beautiful red hair and put it up with pins and clamps. She would put green ribbons in the hair. They snuggled a lot back then.

That was before Mother had started acting differently, had stopped sewing, stopped doing sports, stopped visiting other adults to play cards. She had started doing funny stuff Anneke didn't understand, like yelling in a strange voice and talking out loud to nobody. She'd stood on her head a lot and burned little candles that floated in pots of water. She had started making smoke in the house. Once the firemen needed to come. That was the first time Anneke had been sent to a foster home.

Now she walked back to the living room. Her package of whittled animals sat on the coffee table.

Taking them out, she placed them side by side, rearranged them, feeling each one carefully for its smoothness. If Elishia were her sister she'd let her play with these animals. With Sheera too. Anneke would be the older sister, the smart one, the one who helped her little sister. She'd show Elishia how to whittle, how to catch a fish, how to teach a dog to do tricks, how to make macaroni and cheese. If Elishia were her sister, Eileen and Larry would have to be her parents. Anneke didn't mind Larry. He had the same hobbies as she did, and it was kind of nice sometimes to have a pretend dad. But Eileen! Eileen wanted too much to be her mother. And Anneke already *had* a mother. If only Mother acted more like Eileen, if only Mother still sewed and played cards with other women. Anneke really wanted to be part of a family. Right now she was nowhere. She hadn't even been found yet! Maybe the searchers thought they'd discover her dead body somewhere, killed by a wild animal.

The phone rang.

Jumping up, bumping her knee on the coffee table, she sent the carved animals tumbling to the floor. Not sure what to do, she waited, letting the phone jingle on before it clicked over to the answering machine.

"Hi, Eileen, Larry. Dr. Sunnybrook here. I just wanted to ask you if, when you find the girl, you would contact me right away. At work or at my home. Give me a call at three—"

"Hello?" Anneke had picked up the receiver and spoken into it without thinking about the conse-

68

quences. Now she stopped. Talking to Mother's doctor meant the adult would know where she was. Anneke would have to leave here, and quickly. Then she thought about the wild animals, the thunderstorm, the cold, pelting rain, the hunger. She wanted to stay, wanted a warm bed and food, wanted people to talk to. She wanted a family. Her mind flashed back to Larry and his haggard face on TV. She remembered the family standing in this living room, Eileen holding the sleeping Elishia while Larry kissed her.

"Hello?" came the doctor's voice. "Is someone there? Is this Larry and Eileen Proost's place?"

"It's Anneke."

"Wonderful! You've been found," the woman cheered.

"No, not yet. But I will be."

"You haven't? What do you mean? Can I talk to Larry?"

"No, he's out looking for me."

"Can I talk to Eileen, then?"

"No, she's at my trailer."

"So you are at their place?" the doctor asked. "Alone? Stay on the line and—"

"I'll visit Mother tomorrow morning," Anneke interrupted. She hung up. Gathering her wooden animals, she said, "Come on, Sheera. Let's put my things on my dresser. It's time to fix up our old room. We'll stay here until Mother is better. It probably won't be all that long. Hiding isn't fun anymore."

CHAPTER 5

Anneke woke up to Sheera's happy whining. Before she could rub her eyes, she was lifted and almost crushed in a huge embrace by Larry. Then Eileen hugged her more gently, but longer, much longer. Anneke couldn't see anything, her face pushed against Eileen's shoulder. Eileen rocked her a little, murmuring, "Oh sweetie, oh sweetie, you're safe."

Anneke was strong and could pull herself away from Eileen's embrace—if she wanted to. She didn't. She was found. She was no longer nobody. No longer nowhere. A huge sigh, swelling like a cloud, built up inside her body and escaped into the room.

Then she stiffened. She was never lost! Never *nobody*. When Anneke felt the arms around her loosen, she announced, "So I decided to stay here for now. If that's OK. You invited me before."

"Yes. Of course. Sure. Yes. We're so glad to have

you." Both adults talked at once. Eileen rubbed her eyes; Larry blew his nose.

"How did you find out I was here? Did Dr. Sunnybrook tell you?"

"Yes," Eileen said.

"The search parties are still coming back out of the hills," Larry said, clearing his throat. "I just happened to be down at your trailer when the call came on the radio phone."

Anneke looked at the clock. 11:02 p.m. It hadn't taken them long to get here after the phone call. She had gone to bed right after that, around 10:45. "Was the trailer the search headquarters?" she asked, yawning.

"You could say that," Eileen said. "We kept the food there, and the maps and plans. The searchers regrouped from there."

"And my cave?" Anneke looked from one face to the other. "That's *my* place, you know. Mine and Sheera's." She stood straight and tall, her shoulders back.

"Of course," Larry said, giving her shoulder a little squeeze. "I figured that. I put the lock back on and hid the door behind branches. Tomorrow I'll show you how to put a better lock on the door. That one's no good. It's too easy to open."

"Thanks." That's why she liked Larry, Anneke decided. He got things done, like she did.

Eileen suggested they all have a snack before going to bed.

"I ate the cake," Anneke warned.

"All of it?" Larry laughed. "How you stay so skinny is beyond me."

"Where's Elishia?" Anneke asked.

"At her grandparents'. I was thinking more of big mugs of hot chocolate," Eileen said. "Elishia and her grandmother made that cake for you, in case you came by. I'm glad you liked it."

"I liked it all right. I was starving." Anneke patted her stomach.

"I bet," Larry said. "You're amazing. Just amazing." He shook his head slowly, staring at her.

Anneke smiled, rumpling the hair on Sheera's head.

The next morning she didn't wake up until after ten o'clock. Lying in bed, Anneke thought about living here again, at Larry and Eileen's, in the same room as before. This time, though, she was old enough to take care of herself and make her own decisions. Others could no longer expect her to do things like go to bed early or eat any kind of food they put on her plate. She reached down and petted her dog, then lay back with her arms behind her head. Dreamily, she thought about the cave: her own place, her freedom. The wild forest didn't seem so wild and scary from here. She wanted to fix the fish trap. Maybe spend the day with Ken and go for a swim with Sheera.

"Today, first I'll visit Mother, then we'll get Ken and go to the lake," she told the dog. "Larry and Eileen need to understand that I can look after myself, so they won't come searching for me again."

Anneke got up, let Sheera out, and went to the kitchen for breakfast. Eileen sat at the table with her coffee and newspaper.

"Good morning, sweetie. Did you sleep well?"

"Yes." Anneke stretched. "I'm going to visit Mother. Then I'm going up to my lake and—"

"Let me call Larry," Eileen interrupted, folding her paper. "He's out in the garden. We need to talk."

"What's to talk about?" Annoyed, Anneke sat down at the table.

"You. And we all need to eat breakfast. We waited for you." She called Larry and let Sheera in at the same time. "Your dog has scabs from big scratches," she said. "We noticed them last night. What happened?"

"A cougar." As if facing the wildcat again, Anneke puffed up her body. Cougar, play big and brave. But adults—play big and brave too?

"A cougar?" Larry said, walking in. "Did you say a cougar? You mean there's one up there in the hills, that close to your trailer?"

"At the lake. A bear, too." Anneke relaxed a little. She looked at Larry, then at Eileen. "I'm going up there today. I live there."

"No, sweetie, you live here now. You can't go back there." Eileen gave Sheera a dog biscuit.

"I'm old enough to look after myself and my dog," Anneke started. "I've decided—"

"The government decided differently," Larry interrupted. "Listen up." They all sat at the table, looking at each other. "And listen good," he added firmly when Anneke shrugged her shoulders and made a face.

Larry explained that the case workers were upset about the whole situation. His voice slowly got louder and angrier. "You cost them thousands of dollars, not to mention the huge amount of stress on us all. Sending search and rescue out like that is a big deal. You acted very irresponsibly, not letting anyone know where you were. You say you're old enough, then *show it!*"

He paused, lowered his voice back to its normal pitch, and went on to explain that around nine o'clock that morning a worker from Children and Family Services had arrived to take her away. The worker wanted to put her in a new foster home in the city. "It took a lot of smooth talking and even signing a paper before the woman would agree to let you live here for now," Larry said, leaning forward. "As it is, Eileen and you and I have to go to a meeting next week for further talks. So we are responsible for you. You live *here* now, and that's all there is to it." He placed his hands firmly on the table, fingers spread. "Either here or they'll cart you off to the city. You are too young to live on your own."

"We got along so well before," Eileen said. "We really want you here." She put her arm around Anneke's shoulder.

Anneke shrugged it off, scared and defiant all at

once. "You're *not* my mother," she spit out, surprising herself. "I *have* a mother."

"Of course," Eileen said.

"Nobody cares about Mother. She's just put away!" Anneke shoved the table. Her chair crashed to the floor as she ran out of the kitchen and up to the bedroom.

"Who do they think they are," she muttered to her reflection in the mirror. "I don't need *anybody*."

Sheera whined softly at the door. Anneke let her in. "I do need you, though," she said, sitting on the floor and hugging the animal to her.

Life would be so lonely without Sheera. Larry and Eileen had given her the dog. Anneke remembered the farm they'd visited, the tiny puppies that had tumbled and played and sucked milk from the mother dog. Eileen had said, "You pick any puppy you want. It'll be your very own pet."

Anneke had chosen the one with a little patch of pink skin around the nose, the one who jumped up into her arms and licked her face as if to say, *Take me, I'm cute*. And she had been a cute, wriggling little bundle of black and white fluff.

Eileen had driven them back to the farm a few weeks later to collect the puppy. She had suggested maybe Anneke would like to give her puppy a Dutch name, since her own name was Dutch. They had taken Sheera to the vet for shots, and as soon as the puppy was old enough Anneke had started obedience classes with her. Back then Eileen used to help clean up the messes Sheera made in the house. Eileen. A substitute—for Mother. "Eileen and Larry are just substitutes, only until Mother gets better," Anneke mumbled.

She went back to the kitchen, her pet in tow. "Don't call me sweetie," she stated, her hands on her hips.

"I'm sorry," Eileen said, a slight smile skimming across her face. "I'm so used to calling Elishia that. I'll try to remember."

"Let's have breakfast," Larry said. "Since there is no chocolate cake left," he winked at Anneke, "I guess we'll be forced to eat healthy stuff." He made a gagging sound.

"Macaroni and cheese would be fine," Anneke said.

"Don't tell me," Larry laughed, "you're *still* on your macaroni and cheese kick."

"How about you make that for us for supper tonight," Eileen said, "and I'll barbecue some chicken to go with it."

"Don't tell me you're *still* on your barbecued chicken kick," Anneke grinned.

"Good one." Larry laughed loudly as Eileen pretended to chase Anneke around the table with the frying pan.

Sheera barked as if to say, *I see things haven't changed much after all these years.*

As they walked into the hospital, Anneke remembered being seven and visiting Mother in a special adult group home. Back then one of her foster parents had always come with her. Now Eileen asked again, "Are you sure you don't want me to be there with you?"

Anneke shook her head. "She's my mother. I'll visit her by myself."

They took the elevator to the fourth floor. As they scanned the numbers on the doors, a nurse came towards them. "Who are you looking for?" she asked.

When the nurse had led them to the right room, Anneke said, "See you downstairs." She waited until both adults had left before opening the door quietly. Mother sat on the bed, dressed in her housecoat, looking pale and even skinnier than before the accident. Her right leg was in a cast from the knee down.

Anneke hurried up to the bed, arms ready for a hug. But her mother shrank back as if her daughter were a stranger who might hurt her. "Yes, yes, evil has come," she whispered.

"I'm here for a visit." Anneke stopped before she reached the bed. She noticed Mother's hands shaking more than usual. "How are you?" she asked, taking another step forward. She spread her arms out for a hug again, then as Mother shrank back, let them fall down along her sides.

"Do you want to go home?" she asked. When there was no reply, only a stare, she added, "Are you afraid here?"

"Evil came. Beware of evil," her mother mumbled so softly Anneke almost missed it.

At that moment the door opened and Dr. Sunny-brook walked in. "Hello, dear, how nice of you to come," she said cheerfully.

"I said I would." Anneke noticed Mother hobbling to the far corner of the room. There she sat on the floor with a thud, wrapped her arms around the knee of the good leg, and started rocking back and forth. The cast stuck out like a giant white club, ready to fight the imaginary evil.

"Mother doesn't like it here," Anneke said. "I'll take her home."

"No, not yet," the doctor replied. "Your mother needs to go to a special place in the city for a while."

"How long? What kind of place?"

"A special hospital. She'll get better care and medication."

"How *long?*" Anneke asked again.

"We're not sure." The doctor looked at the woman who sat on the floor, rocking and mumbling as if the discussion didn't involve her.

"Well, a week maybe?" Anneke tried.

"No, dear, at least a few months." The woman came towards Anneke. "You're in a good foster home. Your mother knows that, and it helps."

"How does that help her?" Anneke scoffed.

"To know you're safe. You're loved and wanted. That helps a lot." The doctor nodded vigorously at each of them in turn as if to convince them both.

Anneke put her hands on her hips. "I'm taking her home. She's my mother and . . ." Her voice trailed off. Mother had shrunk back, looking almost like a ghost who was trying to melt away through the wall. She could *not* come home. Anneke herself could not go home either. The adults wouldn't let her live by herself in the trailer, or in the cave. She was a foster child again, stuck at Eileen and Larry's. Rushing out of the room, she sprinted along the hallway to the exit sign, hurried down the four flights of stairs, and sped through the reception area. Eileen sat waiting. "Let's go," Anneke yelled, hardly slowing at the door and running to the parked truck.

A few minutes later Eileen slid in beside her. "Sweetie, I hope—oh, sorry, I called you sweetie again. That'll take some practice. Is everything all right?"

"Yes." Anneke folded her arms across her chest and clenched her teeth to keep herself from crying.

"Your mother and you can have visits sometimes. I arranged that with Dr. Sunnybrook."

"Did you arrange *everything?* She's *my* mother. Mine!" Anneke spat the words out, wishing she could steal Mother away and have them live as a family somewhere far off in the mountains, just she, Mother, and Sheera.

"This must be hard for you. But your mother can't cope right now. You know that," Eileen tried.

"I cope for her. I give her medication and then she's fine." Anneke would not give up that easily. Deep down she knew Eileen was right, but still . . .

"You can't give her a pill if you don't know when she took the last one. Medication must be taken regularly. And you're only eleven. You need to have fun with other kids your age. Not look after your mother."

"I can!" Anneke pressed her back hard against the truck seat and pushed tight fists down on her thighs.

Eileen's hand came to rest on her shoulder. "You're strong and mature for your age. But you're missing too much."

"Like what?" Anneke scoffed. She could easily slide out from under the woman's hand if she wanted to.

"Like camps for preteens. Making things. Going for hikes. Having friends over."

Anneke swallowed the word "boring" she'd planned to yawn. Ken had told her he was going to a soccer camp for two weeks in August. Some of her other classmates had made plans for the summer too before school was out. They all seemed excited when the holidays started.

"Larry has some ideas," Eileen said. She put the key in the ignition and turned the motor on.

"Wait." Anneke wanted to run up to her mother's room, wanted to talk to her. What could they talk about?

Eileen pulled the key out again. "Let's go up and say goodbye one more time. We'll make arrangements for your mother's visit."

Anneke nodded. Silently they went back to the room. Dr. Sunnybrook was still talking to Mother, who sat on the bed, crying. Eileen told her why they'd come.

Anneke walked closer. "Does your leg hurt?" she asked, looking at the big, white cast.

Mother didn't look up.

Dr. Sunnybrook said, "The leg will be fine. It's broken. But the bone is healing and doesn't really give her much pain anymore."

They talked about a possible visit in August, towards the end of the summer holidays. Anneke wanted to hug Mother goodbye. She walked to the bed, but her mother backed away.

The doctor came over and hugged Anneke instead. "This is what your mom wants to do," she said. "But right now she can't. She loves you."

For a moment Anneke rested her head against Dr. Sunnybrook's shoulder. Then, pulling herself free, she blew a kiss from her hand in Mother's direction, the way she'd seen Eileen do with Elishia. She walked out of the room, her throat feeling sore and full.

They left the hospital and drove to the trailer to get extra clothes, Anneke's tool kit, and her sleeping bag. While passing Ken's neighbour, Anneke remembered the borrowed bicycle. Eileen agreed that they needed to return the bike right away. They decided to take the whittled duck as a gift as well.

The man and woman who came to the door of the house were angry, first at Anneke for taking what wasn't hers and then at their daughter for leaving such an expensive bike out on the lawn overnight. But when Anneke said she'd carved the duck herself and they could have it, they smiled.

"Are you that girl who was in the paper?" the

woman asked. When Anneke nodded she added, "I'm glad you're safe."

"Isn't this something," the man chimed in. "A really nice duck. Real smooth." He turned the carving over in his hands.

"Thank you," the woman said. "We'd love to have it."

Anneke was about to climb back into the truck when Ken came walking down the road.

"They found you," he said to Anneke before glancing shyly at Eileen.

"No, they didn't. I decided to come back out. Let's go to Fish Lake. Oh, guess what? It's called Lustre Lake."

"I have to ask my mom." Ken seemed unsure. "I don't know if she'll let me," he added in a whisper.

"Why not?" Anneke whispered back, glancing over her shoulder at Eileen.

"She found out about me playing up there with you. And about the food I took to you. She was *really* mad."

"I stayed in the forest during the thunderstorm." Anneke put her hands on her hips.

Ken's eyes got big. "Really? Give me your phone number. I'll phone you later."

They exchanged numbers, Anneke needing to ask Eileen for hers. It would be the first time ever that a friend would phone for her, Anneke realized. At home they never had a phone—Mother was afraid of voices coming from a receiver.

CHAPTER 6

When Anneke got back from the hospital visit, Larry was putting up a scarecrow in the garden. "You have the darndest dog," he laughed.

"Why? What did she do?" Anneke turned to greet Sheera, who barked at her playfully.

"She ate my strawberries!" Larry shook his head, still grinning. "I found a few ripe ones and put them on the tree stump. That silly mutt ran right over and *ate* them."

"Of course. You have to say 'leave it' if you don't want her to touch them."

Larry made a face. "A dog? Strawberries? I can understand a juicy steak—but strawberries?"

"Oh, yes." Anneke petted Sheera. "She loves berries, thimbleberries, saskatoons, blueberries, whatever. She eats them right off the branches. Probably her favourite fruit is an apple, though."

Larry laughed loudly now. "If I hadn't seen it with my own eyes I'd say you're—" He stopped, then asked, "How's your mom?"

"Fine." Anneke sat on the tree stump and looked at her shoes. Then she added, "Not really. She'll be gone again for a long time. We planned a visit for the end of August."

"Let's make sure it's a nice visit." Larry looked thoughtful, then pointed to an old shed at the far end of the garden. "How would you like to have that shed as your workshop? Then when your mom comes to visit she can stay in your room and you can sleep there. We'll move everything from your cave into it."

"No!" Anneke had liked the idea of a workshop, but now she felt trapped. "No," she said again, shaking her head vigorously. "The cave stays the way it is."

Larry walked over and sat on the lawn beside the stump. "The owner of the trailer phoned. He's not getting paid this month, so he wants to rent the place to someone else. That means you have to move out. After that you can't go back there."

"But it's *mine*. It's where I live. It's . . ." Anneke looked at him, frantically searching his face for a sign that he was joking.

But Larry sat quietly, watching her, not arguing, not jesting. That scared Anneke even more. "He *can't*," she said. "It's our home. When Mother comes back . . ." She cleared her throat, looking at Larry, wanting him to do something. She wanted him to say they could keep the trailer, to say things would go back to how they had been. But she knew they wouldn't.

After a long silence Larry put his hand on hers and said, "You know your mom has schizophrenia, don't you?"

When Anneke nodded, he continued, "When you lived here before, we didn't think you were old enough to understand, but I feel that you are now."

He stopped and she nodded again, waiting.

"Schizophrenia means your mother's brain doesn't always work like ours."

"I know that," Anneke interrupted. "But she can take medication. It fixes everything."

"It's not that easy," Larry said. "The medication might need to be changed at times. It works differently for different people."

"You mean," Anneke said in surprise, "there are other people like my mother?"

"Oh, yes. Many. About one in every hundred people has schizophrenia. Most of them are fine if they take their medication. They lead normal lives." He patted her hand. "Some, like your mom, have a problem for a while. Then they need to be in hospitals or group homes. Your mom will go to a special hospital in Trail to try new medication. Right now she's not well. She hears voices that tell her things."

"Yes," Anneke said. "She says the goddess tells her to do stuff, like make little fires."

"Exactly," Larry said. "And that's dangerous."

"So," Anneke asked, "does that mean when Mother gets the right medication she'll be OK again and we can live in the trailer like before?"

Larry shook his head. "Your mom is confused.

Even with the right medication she will have a lot of other things to work out with a counsellor."

When Anneke said nothing, he added, "I'm very sorry. You won't be able to go back to the trailer."

In the silence that followed, Anneke cried, "Sheera!" The dog came immediately, pressing into her arms, against her body, licking her face. She held the animal for a long time, her head buried in the soft fur.

Finally she said, "*You* are my family." Sheera licked her face once more as if she understood. "Could I get schizophrenia too, because of Mother?" Anneke kept looking down while she whispered the question.

"You have no bigger chance of getting it than anybody else."

"When Mother comes back from the city," Anneke said slowly, still not looking at Larry, "we'll rent some place. I'll be in grade six by then. I can look after things."

Larry didn't respond.

"And Fish Lake, I mean Lustre Lake?" she asked.

"The lake is too dangerous if there's a cougar," he said. "And a bear. We can't let you go up there. Although it doesn't belong to the trailer owner."

"The cougar left. I scared him away," she said, wondering if that was true.

"Maybe." Larry nodded, his face serious. "Cougars wander over large areas. Tell me what happened."

Anneke explained how she and Sheera had

finished eating berries when the cougar had attacked and how together they had fought him off.

With a big frown on his forehead, Larry said, "And you went back up there the next day? Don't you have *any* fear? Or brains?"

She just shrugged in answer.

"You were lucky," he said.

"I clouted him across the eyes so hard, I busted a big stick," Anneke bragged.

"Yes, but still, you were lucky. Cougars are very dangerous." After a short silence he added, "They have killed people, strong adults." He stared straight at her, sighing, "I thought you had more sense."

"I know." She looked at the scar running across the dog's chest and leg. "We *were* lucky," she mumbled. "But we liked it there, didn't we, pal?"

Sheera panted in the heat of the sun, her tongue hanging out of one side of her mouth.

"I'll phone the conservation officer and report the attack," Larry said. "Someone will go up there to check the area out."

"Sheera's hot." Anneke stroked her pet's heavy black coat and added, "At the lake she went in for swims all the time."

"I can take you to the beach at the river for a while."

"Maybe I could just keep the cave without the trailer," Anneke tried.

Larry shook his head. "I'm sorry. This shed will have to do. We'll make it private. We can build a tall fence in the front and plant a few shrubs around it. That reminds me, how would you like to go to a GETT Camp?"

"A *what* camp?"

"A camp where girls learn how to do carpentry. GETT stands for Girls Exploring Trades and Technology. You make go-carts."

The name sounded complicated, like some kind of boring lesson. "I already know how to do carpentry." She thought about Ken and his soccer camp. "Who else goes?"

"Girls who like to do the kind of stuff you do." Larry laughed and added teasingly, "Believe it or not, there are other girls like you."

"You mean girls who like to use tools and make things out of wood?"

"Exactly."

"Sure." Anneke decided she'd give it a try. "Do you think if I paid the trailer owner some rent each month he'd let me keep the cave?"

Larry shook his head. "This is it, kid." He pointed to the small wooden building. "We'll make the place into a real workshop."

"It won't be the same," she shrugged.

"Nothing ever is." He got up and walked to the shed. Slowly, Anneke followed.

After a swim, Anneke spent the rest of the afternoon cleaning out the old shed. Larry helped until he had to leave for his night shift as a psychiatric nurse.

Anneke completely emptied everything out of the shed. Then, sitting on the dusty floor in the middle of the space, she looked around at the four thin, wooden walls. This flimsy shack was not at all like her cave with its big boulders, so strong, so secure. Outside her old hideaway the world could change, go wild, but inside things stayed quiet, safe, and secret. Here, however, light flooded in through two dirty, cobwebbed windows and through cracks and holes in the walls. This wooden structure had no chimney for her barrel stove. The dry boards would likely burn at the first strike of a match anyway. Her belongings from the cave wouldn't fit here. This dump was all wrong.

"Anneke, telephone," Eileen called.

Leaving the shed door wide open—why bother closing *this* space—she ran to the house. That would be Ken on the phone. He'd kept his promise.

After they greeted each other he said, "Tell me about the storm."

Excitedly she related the story about her night alone in the forest, about the thunder and lightning, the swim in the dark, the return to her cave on the flooded path. She left out the part about her bathing suit clinging to her face and scaring her.

Ken kept saying "Cool" or "No way!"

Anneke grinned. "Do you want to help me fix the old shed?" she asked.

"What old shed?"

"The one at Larry and Eileen's. I can't use my cave anymore."

"Why not?" Ken questioned. Then he mumbled, "Oh, I guess . . . uh . . . I have to ask my mom if I'm allowed to come over. I mean, uh . . ." There was a silence. Then he said, "I'll ask my mom."

Anneke waited until Ken picked up the phone again. "I can come for a little while tomorrow morning," he said.

They decided he would ride over on his bike the next morning around ten. Anneke told Eileen about the plans they'd made.

Eileen sighed. "You need to check that kind of thing with me first," she said. "You're a member of this family now. We have to plan together and ask the others if it's convenient to invite someone here. And also if you want to go somewhere."

Anneke's mouth dropped open in surprise. "I'm eleven years old, you know," she said, turning and heading for the front door. "I can make my own plans."

"Just a minute." Eileen stopped her. "I know you can. But there are four of us living here. We all need to be considerate of each other."

"I know, I know. We'll just stay in the shed. He won't even come in the house. Don't worry."

"It's OK this time," Eileen said. "And your friends are always welcome in this house, of course. But check with me first next time, all right? Or with Larry."

"I'm not a baby," Anneke muttered under her breath as she went out to take Sheera for a walk. Then she remembered that Ken had put the phone down during their conversation to check with his mother about coming here tomorrow. He always checked things with his mom. And he was older.

Anneke had started down the driveway with her dog when she heard her name. "Yes?" she called.

"Where are you going?" Eileen asked.

"For a walk. Sheera's bored." She rolled her eyes at the dog as if to say, *Does this woman have to know everything?*

"It's almost time to start supper," Eileen said. "You promised to make macaroni and cheese. I'm turning the barbecue on soon for the chicken."

"So, turn the stupid thing on," Anneke mumbled. "Fine," she said in a louder voice.

"Don't go too far." Eileen started back into the house.

"We won't." Anneke walked down the driveway. Before reaching the bend, she looked over her shoulder. The front door had closed. Heading down the country road, she felt as if they'd just left prison. "Let's run." Sheera didn't have to be told twice.

When they got back, Elishia had just been returned by her grandmother. The little girl looked shyly at Anneke, then put out her hand to pet Sheera when Eileen encouraged her to do so. When Sheera licked her knee, Elishia laughed, her brown eyes shining in her round face.

"She remembers you from last year," Anneke said. "Where's the macaroni?"

While Anneke measured the ingredients, Elishia pulled a chair over to the counter. She kept wanting to look in the pot and help stir. Anneke didn't know why, maybe the element was turned up too high, or the pot's bottom was too thin, but somehow a thick layer of macaroni and cheese burned to the bottom. Setting the smelly mess down on the counter, she said, "*Forget it*. Nothing works today."

Eileen told her not to worry, there was plenty of macaroni still good enough to eat. Putting three plates on the table, she heaped unburned spoonfuls onto each and set the pot aside to soak overnight.

Placing a bowl of tossed salad on the table, she sat down and said, "Did you know that my mom and dad live in this valley now, too? They moved here last year, to be closer to their granddaughter. They'd like to meet you."

"Oh," Anneke said, her mouth full.

"What do you think about inviting them for dinner tomorrow? Larry will be back from work. He said for us to go ahead and make plans." Eileen cut some meat for Elishia.

Anneke took a chicken leg and chewed on the crispy, barbecued skin. Ken was coming tomorrow. She wanted to go to the lake with him to fix the trap but knew neither of them would be allowed to go there again. "Sure," she mumbled between mouthfuls. "Whatever."

"Whatever," Elishia said. "I like this mecroni and cheese." She was trying to scoop some slippery macaroni on her fork, then attempted to stab some instead.

"I think you'll like Gram and Grump," Eileen said.

"Wam-a-Wump, Wam-a-Wump," Elishia chanted, trying to pick up some slippery macaroni with her fingers.

Eileen smiled, passing Elishia a spoon. "That's her way of saying Grandma and Grandpa," she explained. "That's how we ended up calling them Gram and Grump. "I think you'll love their outdoorsy life. A few weeks ago they talked about taking us all to the Rocky Mountains this August. Now that you're here, that would include you."

Anneke looked up quickly. "Mother will visit in August."

"Of course," Eileen said. "We'll plan around that. Your mother's visit is most important."

Elishia put her spoon down. "My mother's visit is most upportant too!" She looked from one to the other. Eileen smiled and nodded at her daughter.

"The Rockies sound great," Anneke said. "As long as Sheera can come."

"Oh, yes. She's part of the family."

The next morning, right at ten, Mrs. Uno, Ken's mother, drove up. Anneke noticed her friend grinning, trying to hide his embarrassment as his mother, in a flowery summer dress and red shoes, click-clacked up to the door. Mrs. Uno introduced herself, and Eileen, who had been outside at the sandbox with Elishia, invited her in for coffee.

Anneke followed them. She wondered why Ken's mother had brought him here. Also, the shiny red purse and high heels fascinated her. Her own mother owned only flat shoes and boots.

"Let's go to the shack," Ken whispered, hanging back at the door.

"There's lemonade in the fridge," Anneke said. "It's sweet. I made it."

"OK." He waited.

Anneke watched as Mrs. Uno sat, foot beside foot, high heel exactly beside high heel, red purse on her lap, her hands wrapped around the strap. She smelled of perfume or soap or something. A strange smell, but not unpleasant.

The two women drank their coffee. They talked about the hot weather, about the valley, about how long each had lived here. Slowly, while listening, Anneke poured two glasses of lemonade. She gave one to Ken and they went to the shed.

"My mom wouldn't let me come by myself," he said. "She's checking things out because you're in a foster home now." He shrugged.

Anneke looked straight at him and nodded. At least Ken told her the truth, she thought. Not like others at school, who either mumbled something or ignored her. "Boring adult talk," she said. "Boring life. I wish I was back at the cave and the lake."

Ken agreed. He asked about the woods and the hiding places. He wanted to hear about her adventures again.

Happily she told him, ending with, "Let's go to the woods now."

"No way. With wild animals and lightning and

rain? I mean, it sounds cool that you did all that, but . . ." He stared at her, shaking his head.

They nailed old boards over the holes and cracks in the shed walls. Ken's mom came in to say she'd be back to pick him up for lunch. Eileen gave them leftover cans of paint and brushes to paint the walls: one red, one grey, two brown. Before they finished painting Ken had to leave.

Anneke ate lunch with Elishia and Eileen before everyone piled into the car, picked Larry up, and went to the river for a swim. Anneke showed Elishia some of Sheera's tricks. "Watch this," she said, throwing a stick into the river for the dog to fetch.

"Me too, me too," Elishia cheered, flinging a rock into the water.

"No, no, it has to float," Anneke said, giving the little girl the stick Sheera had just brought back. After playing fetch for a while, Elishia wanted to be pulled through the water by holding onto the dog's tail. Sheera allowed it only for a short while before she swam to the edge of the water. The two girls built a castle, Elishia making a pile of sand with her little plastic bucket. Anneke dug a moat and filled the hollow with water. They worked hard until Sheera sat on top of the castle.

"Bad dog," Elishia said. She threw a handful of sand in Sheera's direction.

"It's all just beach to her," Anneke explained. "Animals don't know any better. Here, cover up my legs." She lay down with her feet in the castle's moat. Elishia covered first her feet, then her legs, then all the way up to her shoulders with buckets full of sand. When Elishia started pouring water on her, Anneke growled and pretended to be an angry animal. The little girl ran into the river and splashed water all around her. The two played and swam until Larry called, "Time to go home for dinner with Gram and Grump. I'll barbecue the salmon, you women make a salad."

"Potato or green?" Eileen asked.

"I can make Dutch potato salad," Anneke said. "Mother showed me."

"You're on," Eileen smiled.

When they piled into the truck, Elishia threw her arms around Anneke and wanted to sit on her lap.

While Anneke put the last silver onion on the salad, Elishia called "Wam-a-Wump, Wam-a-Wump." A woman and a man stepped out of the car in the driveway.

Grump didn't look at all grumpy. He had a shiny, bald head, a pointy grey beard, and twinkling eyes. He picked Elishia up, tossed her in the air, and caught her in a bear hug, whooping, "Hello, my pumpkin pie. How are you?"

The little girl squealed. She kissed the top of his head and found a candy in the pocket of his short-sleeved shirt. While Elishia was still in Grump's arms, Gram kissed her as well.

Anneke had expected Gram to wear an old-fashioned dress and glasses. Instead she had short, straight hair, wore lipstick, and sported a T-shirt that read *10 km Run. I did it!* Between her khaki hiking shorts and running shoes were strong, brown legs. Neither Gram nor Grump looked any older than some of the teachers at school.

Everyone hugged and greeted each other, all except Anneke, who stayed back and watched. Now they turned to her.

"You must be Anneke," Grump said. "We've heard so much about you." He shook her hand.

"We finally get to meet you," Gram chimed in. For a second it looked as if she was going to hug Anneke, but then she put out her hand.

"She made a Dutch potato salad," Eileen said. "What am I saying, it isn't just a salad, it's a plate full of goodies almost too beautiful to eat."

"This is one talented young person, if you ask me," Larry added. "Maybe she'll show you some of her whittled animals and her new workshop."

"Sure." Anneke shrugged, feeling awkward with all the attention. "Sheera's hungry. I'll feed her." She ran ahead of her dog to the kitchen.

CHAPTER 7

Anneke opened her eyes and looked around in confusion. Where was she? Oh yes, they had spent the night in the new workshop. Sheera lay beside her on a mat, tail thumping on the floor, eyes watching her. For the last three weeks Ken, Larry, Eileen, and even Grump and Gram had helped her fix this place. They had insulated the walls, run an electric cable from the house, and put in a light. On one side under a window stood a sturdy wooden workbench with a second-hand vise, a present from Larry and Eileen. Opposite from where Anneke lay on the floor were a table and three chairs, given to her by Gram and Grump. The flowers Elishia had picked from the garden decorated the table, the stems so short they hardly stayed in the vase. The cooler and dishes from the cave would go in an empty cupboard behind the furniture.

Yesterday they'd all had a party in here, Anneke, Larry, Eileen, Elishia, Gram, Grump, and Ken, whose mother had also been invited but didn't come. She had sent a cake with Ken, though, and a card that said *Congratulations on your new home.* Anneke had wanted Ken to stay overnight, but he wasn't allowed.

She stretched, crawled out of her sleeping bag, and tickled Sheera. They romped for a few minutes before Anneke got dressed. "I think I'll move into this workshop. It's cool," she said to her dog. She remembered that only three weeks ago, when this shed had gaped empty and dirty, she'd left the door wide open. Now this place was no longer a dump, but her own private den behind insulated walls and a fence. Curtains hung on the windows, and shelves for displaying her carvings covered part of one wall. Closing the door firmly behind her, Anneke watered the new shrubs by the fence before heading to the house for breakfast.

Today she and Eileen were going to pack the last of her and Mother's belongings in boxes and clean the trailer. Tomorrow a new renter would move in, the landlord had said on the phone. All items that belonged to the former tenants had better be gone by three o'clock. He would consider anything left as trash and take it to the landfill. He was angry because nobody had paid him any rent for July.

After finishing breakfast everyone rushed around. Larry took Elishia to her grandparents' before going to work. Eileen and Anneke loaded the truck with empty boxes, cleaning materials, and their lunches. They planned to be at the trailer for most of the day.

By early afternoon the place sparkled. "It's a lot cleaner than when we moved in," Anneke said.

"Good," Eileen replied. "Always leave something better than you find it."

"I want to do the cave alone." Anneke ambled through the back pasture, her dog in tow. This was their last hike up here. She looked back at the trailer that stood empty and forlorn in the weed field, baking in the hot sun. "Oh, Mother," Anneke mumbled, her throat feeling full. Sheera pressed against her legs. Sitting down in the tall weeds, she hugged her dog and buried her face in the fur for a minute.

"Come on," she challenged, jumping up. "I'll race you."

As always Sheera won the race, and as always the cave stood cool and dark after the hot sun. Anneke touched the big boulders, the strong walls, the stovepipe, the homemade stove. "I'll miss you," she whispered.

The cooler hadn't been closed properly and the once-frozen orange juice had leaked and soaked all through the other foods. Everything stank. When she dumped the mouldy mess out in the weeds, Sheera sniffed eagerly but didn't eat anything.

Sorting through her few belongings, she packed them one by one into a box. Anneke left the stove, the bed of hay, and the wood for the porch, but gathered up the rope. The latch on the door unscrewed easily. The key to the cave and the padlock landed in the box with a thud. Next she took the trailer key from the ring on her belt. The owner wanted it back. Now only the knife hung on the ring. No keys. "We'll start again," she whispered, tracing the ring with her finger before closing the door firmly behind her.

Back home Eileen made a big, fresh garden salad while Anneke heated hot dogs and beans, stirring with a wooden spoon. Elishia was staying at Gram and Grump's until her bedtime and Larry was at work till the next day.

"Just the two of us," Eileen said, setting the table.

Just the two of them. Anneke and Mother. Beans and sausages, their favourite meal on a hot summer day. Anneke cooking. Mother setting the table, singing and joking. Now Mother was gone. Anneke had Eileen instead. Eileen. Not her real mother.

"You are *not* my mother!" The wooden spoon landed in the sink as Anneke fled from the kitchen. Sheera barked in surprise and hurried after her to the workshop.

Sitting down on the sleeping bag, she noticed her hands were shaking. She wanted to cry but didn't. Wanted to hit something but didn't. She wanted Mother, and the trailer, and her cave. Her arms went around Sheera and hugged tightly. The dog's fur was soft. Anneke slowly rubbed her cheek on her pet's head, back and forth, back and forth.

Eileen knocked on the door. "Dinner's ready. You've had a rough day, with having to say goodbye to your old home."

Staying on the sleeping bag, Anneke said nothing. What was left to say? Yes, the trailer and the cave were gone for good. In her mind she again saw the big boulders, resting on each other. Together they made a safe place. Together. Holding each other.

Anneke got up, opened the door, and walked into Eileen's arms. Eileen hugged her, held her close.

"Oh, swee—sorry."

They stood in silence until Anneke said, "You can call me sweetie if you have to. But you are *not* my mother."

"I know you miss her."

"Yes." Anneke pulled herself free. "When Mother comes back I'm going to make things like they were."

"Your mom is doing a bit better on the new medication."

"How do you know?" Anneke looked up in surprise.

"Dr. Sunnybrook called. She told me."

"And you didn't tell me?" Anneke took a step back. "I'm old enough to be in charge of me and my mother."

"I'm sorry. Not yet." Eileen shook her head as if there was no arguing the point. "This is really hard for you, I know. You are very capable. But this is something adults look after. Dr. Sunnybrook only called just now, a few minutes ago. Of course we'll tell you right away when she phones with news."

Anneke turned and stomped into her workshop. "I'm moving in here," she said, closing the door in Eileen's face. In the cardboard box she found the latch and the padlock that had been on the cave's door. Using the drill, she made holes to put the lock on the door. The key went back onto her key ring.

"Tomorrow I'll find a lock to put on the outside of the door too," she told Sheera. "Then we'll live here until Mother gets better."

With the screws tightly in place and the door locked, Anneke took a new piece of wood. The last time she had whittled was at Fish Lake. That seemed like months ago.

A car door slammed shut. Anneke carved on, ignoring everything outside her own place.

A while later a quiet knock on the door surprised her. "Yes," she called automatically.

"It's Gram. I have something for you."

Anneke unlocked and opened the door.

"How did you sleep in here last night?" Gram carried a tray with a plate of beans, hot dogs, and salad, along with ketchup, salad dressing, two glasses of lemonade, and a package of photos.

"I slept OK." Anneke sat at the table and started eating hungrily. Tomorrow she would need to clean and fill her cooler.

Gram took out the photographs. "The Rockies," she said, explaining each picture. "This is our motorhome. When we go away it'll be big enough for all of us, or if you want to set up a tent beside it, you can have your own space."

Anneke nodded, her mouth full.

Gram put the pictures away and sipped on her lemonade. "I was a loner as a girl," she said. "I still like my own space a lot. Grump and I each have our own room in our house. I spend a lot of time in mine."

Anneke had finished eating. They sat drinking lemonade, not talking.

Finally Gram set her empty glass back on the tray and said, "Elishia wants to show you the pictures she drew for you. She talked about you a lot today and thinks you're wonderful to have around." Gram picked up the tray and headed for the door.

Anneke followed her.

Cars stopped and started, started and stopped at one of Nelson's few traffic lights. Anneke and Elishia sat on chairs behind a table on the sidewalk. On the table in front of them stood a pitcher of lemonade, glasses, and a carved wooden fish, squirrel, and cougar. Only minutes ago a man had bought the whittled dog, saying it looked exactly like Sheera. He had paid five dollars for the carving and ten cents for a small glass of lemonade.

"I'm thirsty. I want more," Elishia said. "Wump doesn't mind."

"He made this lemonade for you to sell," Anneke laughed, ruffling the little girl's hair. "You drank two big glasses already. And," she warned, "there is no bathroom here."

Selling these things had been Grump's idea. He told them that as a kid he'd sold lots of goods to make pocket money. After lunch he'd helped the girls set up at this corner. There'd be more people coming by here than along their own quiet country road. Elishia had sold three tall and four small glasses of lemonade, giving her $1.15. Anneke's sign read *Made to order. Pay what you can. $2.50 to $5.00.* Her customers had bought the dog and a duck. Her pocket now held $7.50 to add to her savings for a CD player she wanted for the workshop.

"I have to go to the baffroom," Elishia whined.

Anneke groaned. Why had she even mentioned that word. The little girl must be getting tired. They'd been here for probably close to an hour. "You'll have to wait," she said. "Grump won't be long now. Start looking for his car." Wondering what time it was, she picked up her knife and continued carving another duck.

Many people walked by. No one else stopped until a woman got off her bicycle and paid for a small glass of lemonade.

"It's hot," she panted, wiping the sweat from her face. "This is a good idea, girls." She picked up the wooden squirrel, studied the curves, then put the carving back on the table and rode on.

"I'm hot." Elishia wiped her forehead. "I want some 'monade."

"We'll go home soon." Anneke saw Mr. Brownwig, her grade five teacher, coming over to them.

"How are you?" he smiled.

"Fine." She continued carving, giving her an excuse not to have to look up at the man.

"Very enterprising." He picked up and examined each animal. "I see you have real talent. I guess you'll do OK."

Anneke nodded. She always did OK.

"I have 'monade," Elishia piped up, sliding back and forth in her chair.

"How nice," the teacher said. He picked up the cougar. "Will you autograph this one for me?"

"Autograph?" She took the cougar from him.

"Yes, you may be a famous carver one day. Who knows. Then I want to be able to say 'I was her teacher, way back when.' You should sign them all." He handed her a pen.

Anneke scribbled her name on the bottom of each carving. Mr. Brownwig put down three dollars. "Thanks," she said.

"Good luck." He walked on, the pen and the cougar sticking out of his shirt pocket.

A little later Grump picked them up. He was excited about their success, as were Larry, Eileen, and Gram. Even Sheera waved her tail proudly. Elishia ran up to her mom excitedly, showing the money in her hand. Eileen smiled at Anneke. Her lips formed a silent "Thanks" as she hugged the little girl. They all had drinks and cookies on the grandparents' deck.

Gram brought out the calendar to plan their camping trip to the Rockies. Larry crossed off his work days in August, and Eileen said that she had two bake sales to organize for the end of the month. They wrote Anneke's carpentry camp dates on the calendar. That left Mother's visit to schedule in. Everyone fell silent until Gram said, "Let's phone her."

Eileen got up. "I'll phone. Dr. Sunnybrook might give us some ideas about dates." She went in. Anneke followed her and overheard the question, then a long silence and "I see." Silence. "Yes, yes." Silence. "I understand."

After hanging up the phone, Eileen sat down, a worried look on her face. "What?" Anneke asked. "What did the doctor say?"

"This won't be easy." Eileen rubbed her lips with a fingertip.

Knowing couldn't be as hard as not knowing. "What?" she said again, loudly, taking a step closer.

"I know how much you were counting on your mom's visit. But . . . well . . ."

Mother wasn't coming this summer. Anneke felt her eyes stinging with disappointment. Squeezing them tight for a second, she asked quietly, "Isn't the new medication working?"

"It's not that." Eileen shook her head slowly. "It's—well, I guess you have a right to know."

Anneke waited, not moving.

"Your mother has refused to take any more medication. She thinks everything is fine with her now. But things aren't OK. Your mom is delusional, which means she believes things that aren't real."

Eileen cleared her throat, then added quickly, "Of course the doctors will get her through this stage. They did before. Things are just taking a little longer than expected."

Anneke clenched her fist. "She *has* to take her medication. I'll go to the hospital. I know how to make her."

Eileen put her hand on Anneke's shoulder. "No, sweetie, you can't."

Anneke walked away, feeling as if the largest rocks in her cave had just crashed down on her. Mother was *not* coming home. She wouldn't come back for a long time. Maybe as long as last time. A whole year, or maybe even longer. That time things had happened exactly this way too. Mother had not cooperated. Anneke could do nothing.

Now she'd be in a foster home all through grade six. Kids would tease her about it. They'd whisper behind her back. Larry and Eileen were OK, Elishia was cute, but this was a *foster* home. I'll live on my own, she thought. I'm old enough. I have a whole month before school starts. I'll make plans.

Last night, plans for the month of August had been made by the four adults. Whenever they had tried to involve Anneke, she'd shrugged and mumbled, "Whatever."

Now, after breakfast, Larry went to work. Eileen, Anneke, and Elishia helped Gram and Grump pack the motorhome for their trip, shopping, cleaning, and sorting. The two girls set up the tent to air it out.

Elishia bubbled on excitedly. "We can have a tea party in here. Wam has cups. I get Wuffie." She ran into the house.

Gruffie was a stuffed sea lion, Anneke knew. She didn't want to play with Elishia. She didn't want to help the adults, didn't care if she went along on the camping trip or stayed home. Just didn't care.

Grump packed his fishing gear. He asked if Anneke wanted to go fishing with him. "Whatever," she said listlessly. Nothing sounded like fun. Mother wasn't coming home for a long time.

On Sunday they all went to the park for a barbecue with Gram and Grump's friends and their neighbours. Four other children came, ages two, seven, twelve, and thirteen. They played Frisbee, soccer, hide-and-seek. Anneke didn't care about being found—she wandered away from everyone. She lay down in the tall grass, Sheera's head on her stomach. The dog stared sadly at her, unblinking.

When she and Sheera finally walked back to the park, the other children had gone on to play badminton. Nobody even missed me, she thought.

"There you are." Gram held out a glass of juice. "Did you go for a walk?"

"Uh-huh," Anneke nodded.

"I want to show you something." Gram took her wallet from her bag and pulled out a very old, wrinkled, grey and white photograph of a woman holding a baby. "My mother and I. Mama died when I was ten. I knew she would never come back, not the way it was before, anyway. But she's been with me all my life. Sometimes I talk to her in my head."

Anneke looked closer at the picture. The woman smiled lovingly at the little bundle in her arms. She looked dreamy, far away. Mama *was* far away.

"I don't usually tell people," Gram said. "They might not understand." She put the picture back in her wallet.

Anneke took a long drink from the glass. Mother would have enjoyed this barbecue. On good days they loved to go to the park and play games. They were great at badminton, lousy at Frisbee. Anneke wandered over to where the other kids were playing tag. "You're it," the thirteen-year-old, George, called, touching her shoulder. She ran after the twelve-year-old, named Mara.

They played until Grump called, "Food's ready." He handed them each a plate and said, "Help yourself, there's lots."

George tried a sliver of barbecued chicken. "Yummm," he said, taking a large piece. "Your mother's a good cook."

"She's not my mother." Anneke took a cob of corn and put butter on it. "But my mother *is* a good cook," she said, remembering that Mother loved corn on the cob. Did the hospital ever have picnics?

When they got home from the park, Anneke went to the basement. Boxes of their belongings stood piled in one corner, covered with white sheets. Pulling down the rickety old table and three chairs, she opened the cardboard boxes under them. They held sheets, towels, pots, pans, dishes, candles, games, trinkets—their life, packed away, put on hold. Straining, grunting a little while pushing at the boxes, she opened lids, pulled out items, threw them around her on the floor. Panting heavily now, she uncovered the bottom boxes. There it lay. The photo album. Mother's treasures from earlier years.

The first picture showed Mother with Bep, her older sister in Holland. Anneke knew that Tante Bep had died when Mother was 21. That's when she had come to Canada, alone, with no family left.

The second photo was of Halifax. Mother, a happy young woman in a yellow chambermaid's uniform, stood with the owners beside the house where she rented a room. The flowers in the gardens looked beautiful. Mother still loved bright and tidy gardens back then.

Next came the train trip across Canada, that long journey from coast to coast, made alone in a new and exciting country. Snapshots taken from the windows, some blurry, showed big old buildings, lakes, rivers, forests, farms, the Prairies, grain elevators, the Rocky Mountains. Most pictures in the album told about this one long trip across the continent. The final shot was taken at a hotel in Vancouver where Mother had worked as a waitress.

I'll keep this in my room with me, Anneke decided. She lifted the rest of the contents out of the box, then wound the key on a very old, tiny music box that used to belong to Tante Bep. Even now the sound trilled like elves ringing little bells. She'd keep this in her bedroom, too.

A pair of small, white gloves lay folded in a soft cloth bag. Mother never said whom they had belonged to. Dried flowers were pressed between pages of a Dutch book. Last, from the bottom of the box, came an envelope with papers from Holland.

The passport tumbled out first. In the photo Mother looked serious, with makeup on her face and her hair curled. The other papers were all written in Dutch. Once Anneke had tried to read them, but she'd soon gotten bored. Reading English had been hard enough back then, never mind Dutch.

Now she flipped through everything carefully, pulling all the papers out of the envelope. Some had fancy letters and stamps on them. They looked official, like certificates. One, written in English, showed Anneke's name on a line and the date of her birth. Clipped to this document was a small picture. The photograph fit in the palm of her hand. It showed a woman holding a tiny baby in her arms, smiling at the baby. Mother and Anneke. Mama and Kindeke.

Mama looked dreamy, far away. She *was* far away. But she was also here.

CHAPTER 8

Very early on Tuesday morning Grump drove the motorhome out of the driveway. The two girls lay cuddled together on the double bed. They giggled, then yawned. From time to time the vehicle rocked gently.

They woke up when Grump stopped for breakfast. Anneke helped Elishia peel her orange. Sheera helped Elishia finish her bowl of cereal. After a splash in the nearby lake they drove on. The day was hot, the drive long. They played cards and other games, sang, drew pictures. Gram had bought face paint, so they decorated each other's faces, making long streaks when the motorhome went over bumps. The four adults took turns driving.

In the afternoon they reached the Rockies. As Anneke looked out the window, she felt Mother's photograph in her pocket. She pretended the two of them were travelling on the train together, talking, pointing out mountain peaks, rivers, and bridges.

"Look," Mother exclaimed. "Bighorn sheep, there, along the side of the tracks." She wanted to stop the train and pet the sheep, but of course they kept on moving.

"I'll take a picture," Anneke said, looking through the camera. "It'll probably be a bit blurry."

"Would you like the camera?" Larry asked.

"Huh?" Anneke looked up in confusion. Mother and the train were gone. The motorhome swerved around a bend as Larry handed her the little black box.

"I saw mountain sheep, back there." She pointed.

"Really?" Larry said. "Next time tell us right away. We might be able to pull off the road and get a good photo."

She nodded. It would be fun to take lots of pictures. She'd show them to Mother someday.

When they arrived at the Banff campsite, Anneke had just enough time to set up the tent before supper. Hamburgers. Biting into hers hungrily, she listened to everyone making plans. Eileen wanted to go for a walk and Gram decided to go with her. Grump planned to take Elishia fishing. Did Anneke want to come? She shook her head. Larry wanted time to relax. He chose to stay at the motorhome and read a book.

"What about you?" Eileen asked Anneke.

"I'll just hang out." She shrugged, feeling a need to be alone after spending the whole day in the motorhome with everyone. "I'll walk Sheera."

"Me too, hang out," Elishia said, dangling a slice of pickle between two fingers.

"Are you sure you don't want to come with us?" Eileen asked.

Anneke shook her head.

"She'll be fine," Gram said.

The next day, and the whole next week, they hiked, fished, sang songs by the campfire, and played games. Gram taught Anneke how to play cribbage. The older woman won most times, counting many points and moving her pegs along the crib board quickly. Anneke liked that Gram didn't just let her win as you would with a little kid. They sat together, not talking much, playing cards, sipping lemonade, each thinking her own thoughts. Sometimes Anneke pretended Gram was Mother. In her head she talked to Mother, told her to look at the cheeky chipmunks that scampered right up onto the table, at the elk that wandered around their campsite once, at the beautiful sunset over the mountains, at the cold, silky waters of the Bow River that just kept moving, kept moving, kept flowing on.

One morning, while the others lingered around the breakfast fire, Anneke found a promising chunk of wood at the firewood bin. There'd hardly been time to whittle lately, every day was so full of exciting activities. Now Anneke slowly turned the wood, studying the shape, the grain, the knots. Her fingers stroked the smooth side where the shape of an animal's back stood out clearly. An elk maybe, its head bent down to eat. A female elk without antlers. That's what the wood showed her.

The knife carved, carved. When she looked up Gram and Grump stood close by, studying her.

"You do that so easily, even with just an ordinary pocket knife," Grump said admiringly.

Anneke blushed with pride.

"We're going to Lake Louise to rent canoes," Gram said. "You can bring the carving."

Anneke shook her head and put the piece of wood in the tent. As she pulled her handkerchief from her pocket, the picture of Mother fell out. Gram picked up the photo. She glanced at the snapshot briefly but said nothing as she handed the small treasure back. Anneke slipped the picture deep into her pocket, glad the older woman, not someone else, had found it. They smiled at each other, their eyes connecting in their shared secret.

At a Lake Louise store while Grump bought everyone caps to wear, Gram paid for something else. She slipped a small leather wallet into Anneke's hand. Inside was a pocket just right for Mother's picture, a pocket with a see-through plastic cover. Gram said, "It clips to your key ring."

Anneke bought two postcards, one for Mother and one for Ken. Mother's showed a river and a snow-capped mountain in the background. On the card she wrote, "I wish we could see the Rockies together. Get better soon. Then I'll get the trailer back for us. I miss you. Love, Anneke." She felt silly about writing "love" on a card where everyone could read it.

Ken's card went into her pack because she didn't have his address. The picture showed a grizzly bear standing on its hind legs, its mouth wide open, showing big teeth. Ken would be impressed.

As soon as Anneke returned from her trip, Ken phoned to make plans for a get-together. While her friend put down the phone to check times with his mom, Anneke checked with Larry, who nodded. "Be back before supper."

She and Sheera caught a ride with a neighbour. "Thanks," Anneke yelled, slamming the heavy door. They'd be picked up again at suppertime.

She paused for a moment at the beginning of the road, *her* road. This route she used to run along on rainy spring days, saunter along in stifling summer heat, slip and slide along during winter storms. Sheera was already scampering back and forth from weed clump to rock to tree, nose to the ground, sniffing, tail wagging.

"Let's check the cave first." Anneke raced ahead of her dog in the direction of the trailer.

Ken stood waiting outside on his lawn. "Hi," he called.

"I'm going to the cave." She kept running. He followed. She wasn't sure if she wanted him to come. Maybe she wanted to be just with Sheera, and Mother's picture. Maybe she wanted to talk to Mother in her head. Out of breath, they reached the trailer. The mudroom had a fresh coat of white paint, while curtains covered parts of the windows. The weed patch had been mowed very short. Two huge flower pots stood guard by the front door, red petunias trailing so far over the edges, they looked as if they were ready to overrun the entire walkway. A row of hedge shrubs, like patrolling sentries, had been planted along the front of the property. A wooden bird with feet whirling around in the wind quivered on a metal rod stuck in what was now lawn. Mother hated fake birds with whirling feet. Anneke wanted to wring the wooden neck, wanted to rip off the stupidly spinning feet and stomp on them. Instead she just stood there, not moving.

"You should see the inside. It's all redone," Ken said.

Sheera growled, smelling the path to the door. Noticing Ken staring at her, Anneke turned away. Her place was gone, just like Mother. Sharply she called her dog and started back down the road.

"Wait up." Ken hurried after her. "We can go to the cave. My mom's friend rents this place now. I asked her. You can go up there if you want to."

Silently they turned and walked around the trailer to the hill, Sheera running ahead. Then Anneke ran, too, her feet hardly touching the ground. They could still come here! She would talk the renter, whoever it was, into letting her have the cave as her own private place again. She'd put the lock back on the door, go up to the lake, spend the rest of the summer here.

The door stood wide open. The rusty old barrel

still hugged the pipe, but the homemade stove leaned over to one side. The wood for the porch lay on the ground. The air inside smelled musty. She picked up an old apple and threw it out. Ken had been right when he said this place felt cold. Unlike her new workshop, which was warm, comfortable, and not so pitch black at night, the cave was always chilly, summer and winter. Anneke rubbed the goosebumps on her arms before touching the wall of big boulders, cold, hard, ungiving. How could this hideout ever have felt so cozy? Safe, yes, but not comfy.

Sheera wouldn't sit in her old spot. She just walked around sniffing. Ken didn't come in at all. Anneke remembered Larry telling her that nothing ever stayed the same. He was right. This cave no longer felt like a safe refuge—it didn't even belong to her. At least the workshop at Larry's was all her own. The door locked from both sides and only she had the keys.

"Let's go. This place stinks." She walked away, leaving the door wide open.

At Ken's home, Mrs. Uno gave them each a glass of juice and some chocolate-chip cookies before they went up the carpeted stairs and down the carpeted hallway to his big room. As well as a neatly made double bed, it had a desk, a computer, a large trunk with its lid shut, a huge bookshelf full of books, and a couch. Everything looked tidy, as if nobody ever played there.

"My camp pictures." He pointed proudly to a wallboard full of photos. "My mom took all these."

"Your mom came with you?" Anneke stared at him in surprise.

"No," Ken scoffed. "On visiting day. There, that's me getting the trophy for most improved player. Man, was it hard."

"You didn't like camp?" Anneke thought about her own camp that would start next Monday. Now that the date was so close, she didn't really want to go, even though she didn't have to stay overnight. So many people would be around all the time.

Her friend broke into her thoughts and said, "The soccer was hard. But I loved camp. Look." He pointed to a picture of boys around a fire. "That's Ben. A real cool guy." Ken laughed. "One night he stayed in this bunk above me, he peed out the window from his bed. Then stupid Robbie, he tried and missed and it bounced back off the window and got him all wet." Ken roared with laughter.

"Gross," Anneke said, wrinkling her nose. "Did he take a shower?"

Ken laughed. "No. One of the head guys heard the noise and came in and turned the light off. So we all pretended we were asleep."

Anneke felt even more relieved that hers was only a day camp. She looked at the other pictures of boys playing soccer, eating at a long table, doing dishes, and playing games. A whole week of that would feel like an eternity, especially without Sheera to snuggle with at night.

"Here, I got you this." Ken handed her a key chain with a miniature soccer ball.

"Thanks." She dug the Rockies card out of her pack and handed it to him. Ken pinned the picture of the grizzly bear up next to the camp photos.

They went outside and kicked a brand-new soccer ball around on the front lawn until Anneke had to catch her ride home.

As the car taking her to the first day of camp waited in the driveway, Anneke hugged Sheera one more time.

"You be good," she said to her dog. To Eileen she added, "I've never left her alone."

"Sheera's not alone, and you won't be gone much longer than if you were going to school," Eileen said. "Don't worry. Have fun."

Anneke nodded. She *did* worry. What if the camp was awful? All of the other girls would be strangers. Getting into the car, she saw three unfamiliar faces looking at her. "Hi," they all said in unison, as if they'd been practising. "Hi," Anneke replied. Eileen held on to Sheera as the car drove off.

On the way to the college, where the camp was held, the other girls giggled from the back seat. They talked quietly to each other while the driver asked Anneke questions. When she answered "Yes" or "No," the conversation in the front seat soon ended and there was silence. Silence to think in. Silence to feel Mother's picture on her belt and to think that if Mother was home she wouldn't have to go to this camp. She could be home carving or building things by herself.

At the camp the leader introduced herself as Sandra and her helper as Marg. Sandra, a carpenter, showed the girls some pictures of things she had built: porches, sheds, studios, houses. Even as a little girl she'd been interested in building with tools, wood, nails, and screws, she explained. Back then mostly men became carpenters, but that was changing. Now camps like this one, camps for Girls Exploring Trades and Technology, GETT Camps, were held in different towns and cities. "So let's *get* to it," she joked, leading everyone on a tour of the workshop. Anneke couldn't help feeling excited about all the big, electric carpentry tools.

Next they formed groups of three. Anneke and two other girls who also stood alone made the final group. Brenda looked about ten years old. Natalie had a scowl on her face. She wore makeup and looked old enough to be in high school. The three girls didn't talk and sat apart while they ate their own bag lunches.

In the afternoon Sandra explained her plan for making go-carts. She and Marg walked around, helping each group in turn.

"You do it," Natalie said to Anneke and Brenda. "I'm only here because my dad made me."

"You all have to work together," Sandra said, walking over.

Natalie shrugged.

"My sister came here last year," Brenda said. "She

gave me some great ideas for making a really fast go-cart."

Laughter drifted over from another group. Anneke looked at them longingly.

"Here's some paper. How about a name for your group?" Sandra tried.

"The Go Getters," Brenda suggested.

"The Go Away and Leave Me Aloners," Natalie smirked.

Anneke kicked her boot against the chair leg. She knew it. She just knew the camp would be awful. She had two and a half more hours before she could go home for the day, and then there'd be another four days to get through. She studied her new boots—well, second-hand new. They were steel-toed boots, all scuffed up but big, heavy, and safe if you dropped things on your feet. "Steel toes," she mumbled.

"You're kidding," Natalie laughed loudly. "The Steel Toes."

Anneke wasn't sure if the older girl was laughing at her, but Brenda said she liked the name.

"Great." Sandra wrote "The Steel Toes" on top of a large sheet of paper. "Now you can design your go-cart," she said, walking off to join another group.

Brenda started drawing a straight line to show the bottom of the cart. She talked about her sister's camp and how her group had been the fastest in the races.

"You mean we race?" Natalie seemed to wake up.

"Yes, on Friday afternoon. After the barbecue."

"Let's throw this baby together." Natalie grabbed a pencil. "What did your sister do to make hers the fastest car?"

Surprised, Anneke looked from one to the other. She didn't care about winning a race, only about using the big electric tools. Bending forward, she joined in the planning. When the time came to go home, Natalie, with Anneke and Brenda's help, had drawn a sleek go-cart with a colourful design on the sides.

The next day, after lessons on safety, Sandra and Marg handed out carpenter's aprons and everyone checked all the tools in them. They drew their plans onto sheets of plywood, using their tape measures, squares, and carpenter's pencils.

"You've done this before," Sandra said to Anneke.

She nodded, explaining, "I'm a carpenter. Larry taught me all this before."

"Cool," Brenda said. Natalie just kept drawing a straight line across the board.

At lunchtime the three girls sat together and planned the race. Natalie said they should go into training and practise running while pushing something. Anneke told her she ran with her dog every day. The other two girls were surprised to hear that she didn't care about winning, that she only wanted to do the carpentry.

"I'll practise with my sister's go-cart every day," Brenda said.

"I'll train by running uphill for half an hour twice

a day," Natalie declared. "Pushing my bike," she added.

Anneke made no comment. They'll be too tired by Friday, she thought. But once the electric tools started humming, the days flew by. She no longer worried about Natalie's attitude or Brenda's fear of the big, whining saw. "Here, I'll do it," she offered as soon as Brenda hesitated. Anneke didn't practise running, but on Thursday evening she did phone Ken to invite him to the next day's barbecue and races.

"You like the camp, don't you?" Larry asked, a smile on his face.

"I like the big tools," she said. "For sure I want to be a carpenter. So you'll pick Ken up at 11:15? Do you know where he lives?"

"Yes, yes, don't worry. We'll all be there to eat and cheer. How about Gram and Grump?"

"Great idea. They'll love it." She picked up the phone again.

"Ask Grump to bring his new video camera," Eileen suggested.

The next morning in the workshop, when Anneke took out her earplugs and looked up, Grump stood nearby with his camera aimed at her and the go-cart. Ken came up beside him, a smile on his face. The girls were putting the finishing touches on their sleek red, yellow, and blue cart. The side panels showed flames painted by Natalie, who, Anneke had found out, would be in grade six, like her, and who was an artist too. They tested the steering and each of the wheels once more while

Grump moved in for some closeups. The girls giggled but kept working.

"Cool," Ken said. "I wish this GETT Camp was for boys too."

The time had come to put down their tools and move to the barbecue outside. Visitors crowded around the parking lot, eating, talking, laughing. The Steel Toes sat together while they ate. Ken brought Elishia over. She stood by Anneke and whispered in her ear, "Can I have a ride?"

"Later."

A gruff voice said, "So, that's it?"

Anneke looked from the scuffed boots up past dirty jeans, up past a grey T-shirt, dirty and ripped on a big, round stomach, up to a scraggly brown beard, long hair, and a sunburned face. The mouth held a sneer. The nose was big and red. Grey eyes mocked the girls and their go-cart.

None of the girls answered. Elishia pushed closer against Anneke, who put her arm around the little girl.

"I said, that's it?" he said louder, kicking a heavy boot against one of the wheels.

"Yes, Dad." Natalie didn't look up when she answered.

"Let's see you win, then." He turned and walked over to the barbecue, pulling out his wallet.

"That's your dad?" Brenda whispered.

"We should practise," Natalie growled.

Ken took Elishia back to the adults while the girls finished their hamburgers in silence. They took the go-cart to the race route set out on the parking lot.

"Zigzag between the cones," Natalie said. "Brenda, you're the lightest. You get in and steer. Keep the turns tight, real tight."

They practised until Anneke decided to save the rest of her energy for the race. She joined Ken, Gram, and the others in the shade of a tree. A while later Sandra called the race.

"Can I ride now?" Elishia jumped up eagerly.

"Not yet." Slowly Anneke got up from the grass. "We have to race. You can cheer us on."

"Remember, these are fun races," Larry said.

"No kidding!" Anneke looked at the starting line, where Natalie's dad stood waving his arms while talking to the other two Steel Toes.

"Ignore him." Ken followed her gaze.

Joining the others, Anneke helped Natalie push the cart into a starting position at the line. They put on their bicycle helmets.

"There's the newspaper guy." Brenda climbed in.

"I wanna see you move this crate," Natalie's dad bellowed. "Let's see you be good at something."

Larry had walked over. "Who painted the sides?" he asked, taking a closer look. Anneke had told him about Natalie's painting, and about her wanting to be an artist.

"Natalie did," both Anneke and Brenda said together, almost too loudly.

"That's great art," Larry nodded. "Beautiful. You're good." He smiled at the big girl, who looked down and didn't respond.

"Excuse us, gentlemen." Sandra came over with a small green flag. "Could you move to the sidelines. We'll start the race."

Natalie, still looking down, snapped, "A quick start is important."

Suddenly Anneke wanted to win the race—wanted to win for Natalie's sake.

"On your marks."

Concentrating on her hands, her feet, her whole body, Anneke readied herself like a spring at the "Get set" command. Off they went at "Go," bodies straining to start the heavy cart into motion. Running. Swaying around the first cone. The second cone. The third. They moved fast and took the lead.

At the fourth and last cone the go-cart had to make a sharp turn all the way around to head back to the starting line, which had become the finish.

Brenda yelled, "Slow down. I can't stee . . . ahhh . . ." Too late. The go-cart swung over onto one side. For a second it teetered on two wheels, as if the cart would tip right over. Brenda screamed. Using every bit of their strength, Anneke and Natalie managed to push all four wheels back down, but they'd lost their momentum. They were also headed in the wrong direction.

While backing up a little, Brenda managed to steer the go-cart into their lane again, facing the finish line. Anneke glanced around. Some other carts were in trouble as well. One lay tipped over, its driver sprawled on the ground, trying to get up.

One team continued in the wrong direction altogether. Two groups had already turned and were running back.

"Let's *go*!" Natalie shouted.

Anneke pushed, ran, sweat pouring from under her helmet and down her face. "Go, go!" she egged herself on in the excitement, the frenzy.

On the sidelines she noticed Natalie's dad, an angry look on his even redder face, waving his arm as if to dismiss them already. "And I paid for you to come here," he yelled.

Then Anneke saw Gram, Eileen, and Larry clapping, smiling, cheering. Ken and Elishia were jumping up and down with excitement. Grump's face was hidden behind the camera. In a final spurt of hot, draining energy Anneke ran to the finish line, pushing with all the energy she could muster.

"Second," an adult yelled. "The Steel Toes, second place. Nice race, girls."

Breathing hard, her legs rubbery, Anneke slumped down on the side of the cart. Good enough for me, she thought. But was it for Natalie? The big girl walked to the building, grabbed her pack, and followed her dad to a rusty old pickup truck. Ignoring Sandra's calls of "Wait, Natalie, wait," they got in and roared off, leaving a cloud of exhaust.

"We have prizes for everyone." Sandra called the girls together. "The race was just for fun and to show off your go-carts to our visitors. But here we have, for the best teamwork . . ." She reached into a box, then paused while everyone waited expectantly.

"Amber, Gail, and Wanda."

The team that had laughed a lot stepped forward to accept a certificate and prizes. Each got a small carpenter's apron and a tape measure. Everyone clapped. The three winners giggled.

"For the best artwork," Sandra carried on, glancing at the empty space between the parked cars. "Natalie, who had to leave. We'll get this to her." She put aside a certificate, apron and tape measure.

"For the girl with the best ideas on how to make a fast go-cart." Again a pause, then, "Brenda." The same prize was handed out.

"For the best carpenter." Sandra waited. Anneke, her heart beating faster, glanced at Larry. He had a huge smile on his face.

"Anneke."

She jumped forward, thrilled, aware everyone had heard that she *was* a carpenter. The best. Grump had moved closer and was again hidden behind his camera. Proudly Anneke accepted her apron, tied it around her waist, slipped the tape measure into one of its many pockets and the rolled-up certificate into another.

"I carve and sell wooden animals," she said, surprising herself.

"I'd love to see them," Sandra said before continuing with the prizes.

At the end the reporter took a picture of the whole group with the leaders. Everyone cheered. Then the camp was finished. Anneke felt sad to go into the woodworkers' shop for the last time.

"Let me show you what I'd like to have," she said to Larry.

"I hope you sell a lot of animals," he said. "These tools are expensive. I have a feeling I know where you'll go after you finish grade twelve."

Those words stopped Anneke in her tracks. She had never thought about what she would do to become a carpenter. But then a smile slowly spread across her face. "I'll be back," she called, walking out the door.

At the parking lot Brenda, Eileen, and Gram were pushing the go-cart while Elishia tried to steer. "This thing is heavy," Eileen panted. "I can appreciate how hard the race must have been."

"Let's go, Brenda," a woman called.

"My mom said you can keep the cart. We already have one." Brenda ran off.

What about Natalie? Anneke wondered if she would be brave enough to phone the big girl and ask her. They could take turns keeping the cart at their places. She got Natalie's phone number from Sandra.

While Grump taped Gram and Eileen running down the race route with Elishia, Anneke said, "Mother would like to see the video."

"For sure." Grump put the camera away and helped lift the go-cart onto the truck.

There'd be so much to tell Mother, so much to show her when she finally got back.

CHAPTER 9

"Natalie?" Anneke held the phone anxiously, hoping the gruff "Yes" on the line was the girl's voice and not her father's.

"Yes," came the same voice again.

Anneke explained that she was phoning to check about who should have the go-cart.

"Keep that bucket of bolts," Natalie grumbled. "Pile of junk. Who wants it."

Anneke smiled. She, Ken, Elishia, and Sheera had been playing with the cart all week. "Where do you live?" she asked. "Eileen said to invite you over for a race and ice cream."

"I'm grounded for the week," the voice snapped back. "Got to go." The phone clicked.

Today was the last Sunday before school started again and the whole family, Grump and Gram included, sat on the lawn with drinks and chips. "Natalie doesn't want the go-cart," Anneke said. "She can't come over—she's grounded."

The group was silent. Larry shook his head. "That poor kid. I hope . . ." He sighed. "She has such talent."

Anneke heard the concern in his voice and a wave of gratitude swept over her. She was glad she lived here now. She was glad she wasn't Natalie.

Elishia pulled one of Sheera's ears. "I want to ride," she said, letting go of the dog and walking to the cart.

"Invite Ken and his mom," Grump said. "We'll make teams with them and race."

Not only Ken but also Mrs. Uno came over for a visit. After making teams, they each raced down the driveway once and were timed. Gram, Larry, and Elishia won. The adults went back to the deck, while the kids raced some more. Ken sat down at the end of the drive. He panted, "You know that new kid, Natalie. She lives in our neighbourhood. That really dumpy old trailer at the end of our road, the one that was empty for a long time, that's where she moved to."

Sheera stood with her front paws stretched up the tree as far as she could reach. A squirrel, perched on a high branch, scolded and teased her. The dog whined. The kids laughed.

Ken continued, "My mom told me to be sociable and introduce Natalie at school on Tuesday." He made a face.

Anneke wondered why the girl had been grounded and what it was like to live with a dad like that. "Natalie is an artist," she said.

"*You* look after her then." Ken sighed with relief. "You're an artist too."

"I have to go on a different bus now." Anneke didn't look forward to Tuesday—a new driver, different kids, a new teacher. And probably lots of homework. "You'll just sit in a corner of the playground and read a book, or play soccer with the boys," she said, glancing at her friend.

"No, I won't." He plucked at the grass.

She added, "Maybe Natalie's OK. Maybe she acts that way because of her dad."

Ken nodded. "We can show her around before school." He jumped up and grabbed Elishia, who had been chatting away to herself as she'd climbed out of the go-cart. The little girl laughed while he put her back in and pushed off. Anneke and Sheera followed.

The first day of the school year had started. On her new bus Anneke knew some of the kids from grade five and sat in the back with them. Ken stood waiting for her at the playground. They hung out with Natalie for a short while until the new girl wandered away without a word, leaving the two standing in the hallway.

"Fine with me," Ken said. He had brought his new soccer ball. They played with a few other kids until the bell rang.

Their grade six teacher, Mrs. Wilson, was cool so far. She didn't give any homework right away.

The first week of school flew by, as did another

weekend. On Monday evening, at Eileen's suggestion, Anneke wrote a letter to Mother, telling her about the camp, the holidays, and the start of school. Writing to Mother was difficult. How would she be doing when she got this letter?

"That's enough," Anneke said. "I want to *talk* to her, not write her."

"She'll appreciate your letter, I'm sure." Eileen handed her a stamp.

"Why doesn't she write to me?" Anneke licked the envelope. "I don't even know what's happening to her. It feels like she's been gone forever."

"We'll phone Dr. Sunnybrook," Eileen said. "We haven't heard for a long time. The doctor promised to phone when there were improvements."

"That means Mother didn't get any better at all." Anneke's stomach suddenly felt heavy, as if she'd swallowed something big and hard.

"No, no, not necessarily," Eileen tried to reassure her.

But Anneke shook her head. "I didn't even think about her much for weeks."

"I'm sure things are fine," Eileen said, dialing the number. When there was no answer, she left a message on the doctor's machine.

By the next evening there had not been a return call. The lump in Anneke's stomach got heavier, harder. "What's happened?" she asked gloomily.

Eileen said, "The doctor doesn't work every day and she's out of town a lot. She probably didn't even get my message yet."

But Anneke felt edgy all that evening. The next

day she paid little attention to the lessons at school, didn't finish her work on time, and left the homework in her locker on purpose. Deep in her head a voice kept droning, *Something bad happened*. And Anneke could not turn that voice off.

Arriving home, she greeted Sheera, opened the front door, and yelled, "Hi, did Dr. Sunnybrook phone?"

When Eileen called back, "She didn't phone," Anneke threw her school bag into the hallway, closed the door with a bang, and hurried to her workshop. Sitting on the floor, she chipped away at the carving of the elk she'd started in the Rockies. Her dog lay beside her, chewing on one of the chips. In her head Anneke talked to Mother about the GETT Camp, about becoming a carpenter. A knock on the door almost made the knife slip. "Yes," she called.

Both Larry and Eileen came in and sat down. Anneke tensed. This looked like a meeting. She left her carving on the floor and sat on the third chair when they indicated for her to do so.

"Dr. Sunnybrook talked to Larry at work today," Eileen started.

Anneke looked at her and felt the hard lump in her stomach again.

Larry said softly, "Your mom was moved to a special group home in Vancouver. You knew that."

Anneke nodded.

Larry continued, "Yesterday morning the nurse

found her room empty. They looked for her all day. Then they phoned Dr. Sunnybrook."

"But—" Anneke spluttered. "How—" She saw a tear glistening in the corner of one of Eileen's eyes. The lump in her stomach grew bigger.

Larry took her hand. "Remember, your mom did this before," he said. "They'll find her."

"She thought about you," Eileen said. "She loves you."

"She left a note." Larry handed her a scrap of paper, torn from the edge of a newspaper.

It read, "Dear Anneke, I'm so sorry. I know you are well looked after now. You will have a good life with them. Mother."

Anneke looked from the note to Larry, to Eileen, and back to the note. She read it again, crumpled the piece of paper up, and said, "Things will go back . . ." But she knew they would never be back to how they had been before. "I want to be alone," she said.

"I don't think that's—" Eileen started, reaching out to Anneke. But Larry took her hand.

"We love you," Eileen whispered before she closed the door.

Anneke found her knife and a new block of wood. She carved and carved, with no plan for a design. The knife scraped. The chips fell. Sheera lay close by her side. Both Larry and Eileen stopped in, one with a snack, the other with a glass of juice. But Anneke didn't want to talk, didn't want anything. Only Mother. She wanted Mother to come back and say "I love you." Not write a stupid little note.

Gram came with the supper tray. Silently putting the food on the table, she sat down, picked up the dog Anneke had carved, and held it. Her fingers stroked the smoothness of the wood for a long time. Anneke watched. The hand moved across the wood, then it slowly reached out towards her.

Like magnets, Anneke's fingers pulled towards Gram's. They sat silently, holding hands.

Finally Anneke whispered, "She doesn't care about me."

Gram's hand tightened around hers. "Your mother can't show it right now."

"I want her." Tears filled Anneke's eyes.

Gram stroked her hair. "It doesn't seem fair," she said.

Tears spilled over their lids. Anneke squeezed her eyes hard. Crying wouldn't bring Mother back.

The older woman curled an arm around her. "Crying is good," she whispered. "Sometimes we need a shower on the inside, to wash away the pain."

Anneke let them flow then, those hot tears, running down her cheeks, soaking Gram's handkerchief. She felt tired, tired and heavy. Her eyes closed. Her head fell forward.

"Come," Gram finally said, helping her up. They walked into the house, into the bedroom, the older woman helping to carry the heaviness. Anneke crawled into bed. Gram sat beside her, holding her hand.

The next morning, when she woke up, Anneke felt lighter. The door stood open and Sheera was not beside the bed. Smells of something sweet frying curled up the stairs to tease her nose.

When she got down to the kitchen, Elishia ran up and threw her arms around Anneke's legs. Bending down to the little girl, she received a syrupy kiss on her cheek. Eileen smiled and said good morning. "You missed the bus," she added. "Gram said she'd drive you to school."

"Me too, me too, Wam," Elishia chanted.

Anneke nodded at Eileen. She was hungry and ate four pancakes loaded with syrup, yogurt, and strawberries. Then she took her school bag and rode to school in Gram's car. They didn't talk. At the classroom door Mrs. Wilson smiled. Gram whispered something to the teacher.

Anneke sat at her desk. She did part of her work. At recess, and at lunch, she stood outside by herself.

"Come on, play soccer," Ken tried.

She shook her head. Went home on the bus. Still no news about Mother. Anneke walked Sheera. Ate. Carved. Slept. Went back to school.

At lunchtime Natalie sauntered over. "You got mother trouble." She turned her head to one side a bit, studying Anneke's face. "I got no mother," she added, walking off, her hands in her pockets.

"Why not?" Anneke realized it was her own voice calling after Natalie. In a few quick steps she caught up and walked beside the big girl.

Natalie glanced at her, shrugged, and said, "She left. I can't blame her."

Silently they walked across the playground before Anneke said, "I don't have a dad."

"Who was that guy, then, at the camp?"

"Larry." Anneke leaned against the fence the way Natalie did, one hand on the wire, the other in her pocket. "He's my foster father." She waited for a sneer about her being a foster child. When none came she continued, "I live with Larry and Eileen. Their little girl is called Elishia. She's sweet." Natalie just looked at her, so Anneke added, "And the grandparents were there at the race. They're OK."

"Lucky," was all Natalie said.

"But it's only a foster home. It's not my real—"

"So?" Natalie interrupted. "You wanna live with my dad? I'll trade ya, him for that Larry guy."

Anneke shook her head. "I guess . . ." She didn't know what to say. "Do you have any other family?" she finally asked.

"An older brother. He left too. I'm glad. He was always fighting with me or my dad."

"Do you ever see him?" Anneke wished Natalie had someone in her life besides that gruff man who was her father.

"No. He moved to Toronto, I think." Natalie kicked at a rock. She was wearing shorts, but she had on her heavy steel-toed boots, even on this warm day.

"You can come over to my place sometime. There's always something going on." Anneke wondered if she should have checked that with

Larry and Eileen first, but then she shrugged.

"No, thanks," Natalie scoffed. "Too many people. I'm a loner."

"Same here." As Anneke said that, pictures of her cave, the forest, the beach at the lake flashed through her mind. "It's nice to be alone sometimes, but . . ." She saw Gram, Elishia, Larry, the others. It was also nice to have them around. If only Mother was a part of it too.

A group of grade six boys sauntered over.

"You, big one, you wanna play?" John sneered at Natalie. The look on his face made Anneke press back against the fence.

"Yah, man, you and the new girl. Let's see ya play," Rudy laughed.

"Cool," Greg chimed in. Some of the others whistled and pressed into a closer circle.

They wanted Natalie and not her, Anneke realized, watching John flick a finger against the new girl's cheek. "Come on," he taunted, "come on, come on, big girl." He pushed one of her shoulders.

Quick as a flash Natalie's fist shot out and hit John with a crunch on his nose. He staggered back, giving a yelp of pain. Rudy grabbed Natalie's other arm, bumping into Anneke, pushing her hard against the fence. She pushed back. Hands started slapping, grabbing, punching. Kids yelled. John fell.

Natalie jumped on him and pinned his shoulders to the ground with her knees. "You puny excuse for a boy," she snarled. "You think you can push me around?"

"You, and you, and you," the duty teacher yelled. "To the office. Get up. You too, to the office."

Anneke walked along with Natalie, Rudy, and John until the teacher deposited all four of them on chairs in the principal's office. Only then she noticed that John's nose was bleeding and that Natalie's cheek had a big scratch. Rudy sat silently, looking scared. John hid his face behind the wet towel someone had passed him. Only Natalie looked around unafraid as if to say *Try me. You'll be sorry.*

The principal asked questions, took notes, gave a lecture about fighting on the school grounds. Anneke had never been in the office for fighting before. She knew John had. As the principal talked on about being a good example to the little kids and getting along, Anneke wondered where Natalie had lived last year. Had she gotten into trouble before? Probably. The big girl didn't look a bit sorry.

With shock she heard the principal's next words. ". . . phone your parents to come in and take you home. I'll expel you for the rest of the day only. Not you, John, this is your second fight in two weeks. You'll be expelled for two days. I'll ask your teacher about homework."

Each of them was told to sit on the floor in a different corner of the front office. While the principal phoned the parents, each student in turn had to go to the classroom for their homework. Anneke went last. She avoided Ken's eyes, wondering what he thought about her now, if he still liked her for how good she was at doing things. Mrs. Wilson handed her a page of math. Anneke knew she wouldn't understand the fractions.

Then the teacher said softly, "I'm sorry you're having a hard time right now. Write a story about your trip to the Rockies with your new family."

Anneke scowled as she walked from the room. Had Eileen told the teacher about the summer? Had Larry? Or Gram? No, Gram wouldn't talk that much to others about her.

Returning to the front office, she heard a familiar gruff voice roaring, ". . . out of trouble this time. You'll stay in grade six forever if you keep this up. You won't amount to nothing, just nothing."

When Natalie tried to say something back, her dad cut her off and yelled, "Don't give me no excuses. You're a troublemaker, like your brother. Now *move!*" With that he shoved her so hard, Natalie nearly fell out the door.

A while later John's mother came in. She waited at the front counter in stony silence, glaring, not even greeting the principal or the secretary. John got up with his bloodied towel, grabbed his bag, and followed her out.

Rudy and Anneke glanced at each other. Neither had ever fought at school before. Anneke didn't mind Rudy. He was good at sports. Sometimes she had watched him play soccer with Ken and the others. She wondered again what Ken thought about all this.

Larry walked in the door, said, "Good afternoon," and asked to speak with the principal in private. A few minutes later he came back. "Do you have your homework?" he asked.

Anneke nodded. She couldn't tell from his face or actions if he was at all angry. Not that she cared much. It was unfair to suspend her—she only shoved people away a few times and didn't really fight, not like Natalie and John. But then, she didn't care if she was suspended for the afternoon anyway. She didn't even want to know how Larry and Eileen felt about all this. How would Mother feel? Mother was gone!

"Let's go, then," Larry said, holding the door open and saying goodbye to the others. Anneke breathed a sigh of relief.

They didn't talk much in the car. Larry just said, "I'm sorry you're going through such a rough time. If I can do something to make it easier, let me know."

Anneke thought about the cave and the lake, but knew that without Mother at home and with all the wild animals on the hill she didn't really want to be there anymore. So she said nothing because there was nothing to say.

Larry dropped her off and went to work. Anneke asked if Dr. Sunnybrook had phoned. Eileen shook her head. Reluctantly, she agreed to let Anneke do her homework in her workshop. "When it gets colder we'll have to put a desk in your bedroom," she said. "You can't keep living in that shed."

"It's not a shed. It's a workshop. A *work*shop, I

work there!" Anneke stomped out of the house.

Throwing the homework in a far corner, she started carving another wooden dog. In the middle of the afternoon Eileen came in with a glass of juice and a muffin. She sat down the way Gram had done.

"We need to talk," she said.

"What about?" Anneke kept carving.

"You seem to get along so well with Gram," Eileen said. "Would you like to spend the weekend there?"

What Anneke wanted was to move her life back to before Mother left. She wanted to whittle, to play at the cave with Sheera, to check every once in a while that Mother was in the trailer, doing fine. "I don't know," she finally shrugged.

"Why don't you try it for tonight."

"Sure." Anneke stood up. If Eileen wanted to get rid of her, she'd go.

Elishia came running to her from the sandbox and fell. She started crying.

Anneke picked her up. "There you go," she said, taking the little girl's elbow and kissing it better.

Up in her bedroom she put some things into an overnight bag and waited in the driveway for Gram's car. When she climbed in with Sheera, she noticed that Eileen gave Gram the homework. In silence they drove down the road.

Gram showed her to the guest room where they left the bag and the homework. In the garden the squashes grew big and round on spreading vines.

Gram pointed out the different shades of orange, beige, and yellow, the darker and lighter green. She commented on how long some of the vines were, stretching from the garden plot across parts of the lawn. One vine even grew all the way up into the lower branches of an evergreen tree. Right there, cradled by a branch, sat a squash.

"Do you see that?" Gram pointed. "This one is really far away from the root of the plant. But it belongs. It grows in a different place, not even on the ground. It's held by a totally different living thing, a tree. Still, it's a squash and not a pine cone."

Anneke nodded, her eyes following the long trail of growth.

Gram continued, "This one is special. I almost don't want to harvest it. When I do, it'll just be an ordinary vegetable again."

Anneke touched the round, green squash that bent the branch down with its weight. "That *is* far," she mumbled, taking five big steps along the vine to the roots.

"It's amazing what nature can do," Gram said.

They went to the flower bed to pull weeds and snip off dead flowers.

"When you remove the wilted ones, the new flowers grow better and more beautiful," Gram explained.

Side by side they worked until Grump called them in for supper.

CHAPTER 10

"What's your homework?" Grump asked on Saturday morning.

"Nothing much. It can wait until tomorrow." Anneke finished the last bite of scrambled eggs.

"Let's do it now," Gram said. "I have to write some letters and Grump needs to do his accounts. We'll all do our paperwork together."

They cleared the kitchen table and Grump spread his papers out on his side while Gram put a writing tablet at her end.

"You write letters to people?" Anneke asked.

"Yes. A few. Most of my friends and I keep in touch on e-mail, but old-fashioned letters are nice for special occasions." She opened the pad to show stationery with flowers and butterflies. "I left a lot of my friends behind when I moved here. But we've kept in touch. Grump and I are going back for a visit next month."

"Yes," Grump added. "If I get this money

business sorted out." He took a stack of receipts from a box.

"I'm supposed to write a story about the Rockies," Anneke said. "Do you think I can make it a pretend letter to Mother and tell her about the summer?"

"Great idea! Here, write on this." Gram tore a sheet off the pad.

They worked in silence until Grump finished his accounts and Gram made them a cup of tea. Anneke had written a long letter and started the math. She sighed.

"Tricky?" Grump asked. "Let's see."

Together they worked on the fractions, Grump sometimes cutting up paper and putting pieces together to explain how to add and subtract fractions until, for the first time, Anneke understood the whole process. "Easy," she beamed. "I never got it last year. Mr. Brownwig didn't explain it this way."

When everyone finished, they went to a friend's for an afternoon potluck. The Robinsons lived in a huge house with a beach along the river. Larry, Eileen, and Elishia had already arrived. Rudy was there too with his mom and dad. A bit shyly he said hi to Anneke.

"Did you do the fractions homework?" he asked.

"Grump helped me." Anneke pointed him out.

"I don't get it," Rudy sighed. "My parents don't either."

"Ask Grump. He's good at explaining." Anneke watched as the older man carefully rubbed sunscreen on Elishia's face. The little girl giggled.

Some of the adults, Rudy, Anneke, and two other kids their age played beach volleyball, jumping, running, and laughing. After the second game, hot, sweaty, and gritty with sand, most of them went into the river for a swim. Rudy did nice duck dives, Anneke noticed. Then the older kids helped Elishia and a little boy build sand castles. Finally everyone ate until they felt as round as volleyballs.

"Would you like to stay with Gram and Grump or come home?" Eileen asked.

"Home?" Anneke said. "Oh, you mean to your house?" When Eileen nodded, she said, "I'll stay with Gram until Monday morning."

"Sunday evening," Eileen said. "We'll pick you up."

On Monday morning when Anneke handed her homework to the teacher, Mrs. Wilson asked, "How was the math?"

"Fine. Grandpa helped me."

The teacher looked surprised. "Your grandfather is here?"

"No, not mine, I mean—" Anneke stopped. She didn't want to explain who Grump was. She'd never known her own grandparents. Gram and Grump were comfortable to be around. With them everything fell into place so easily.

Mrs. Wilson nodded at her and walked up to the front while the room filled with students. John's desk stayed empty. Rudy smiled briefly at Anneke, but Natalie sat with a scowl on her face, looking straight ahead.

At recess Anneke walked onto the playground to watch Ken and some of the others in grade six play soccer. Rudy joined the game.

"Boring," Natalie said, her hands in her pockets.

"Oh, hi." Anneke hadn't heard the girl coming up beside her.

Natalie scoffed, "All they do is kick a stupid ball around. Let's kick some real butt. I can't wait for that John creep to get here tomorrow."

"What will you do?" Anneke moved away slightly.

"You'll see. Nobody scratches me and gets away with it."

Looking at Natalie's cheek, where only a tiny scar was left, Anneke said, "It's not bad. My dog had a long gash and—"

"Who cares." Natalie turned and walked away.

When the soccer ball rolled in her direction, Anneke started dribbling the way Ken had shown her.

"You're on *our* team," Rudy yelled. "Pass, pass, I'm open."

Anneke passed.

All that week they played soccer. Anneke had never played with these boys and girls when they were in grade five. But now Ken, who owned the ball, kept asking her to join them. She enjoyed the attention more than the actual game. Unlike Rudy, who was very competitive, she never cared if her team won or lost. She did score a goal once and smiled when the others yelled nice things at her.

Natalie had not talked to her again. Somehow, strangely, Natalie and John were now hanging out together. They had been called to the office once again, this time for bothering some younger children on the playground.

On Friday at lunch Ken said, "My mom is going to have a picnic up at Fish Lake. With Mrs. Bricks, that new woman who lives in your trailer, and your family if you want to come."

Anneke thought about the words "your family," your trailer." How could they both be hers at the same time? "It's not my trailer anymore," she said. "And I have to check with Larry and Eileen. They're my *foster* family."

"I hope you come," Ken said. "My mom's bringing barbecued chicken She puts a Japanese sauce on it."

"They'll come," Anneke grinned. Then she stopped. "The cougar—Larry said we can't go up there again."

"Mrs. Bricks phoned the conservation officer about that. He checked several times, but the cougar and bear never came back. Mrs. Bricks and my mom went up there twice already. They bring a CD player to make noise. They like it up there."

Anneke smiled. "I clobbered that cougar good," she boasted. "Right on the eyes. I wonder about the fish trap."

Ken took his soccer ball from his locker. "Let's play," he said. "I'll phone you tonight."

On Saturday afternoon Anneke and Sheera walked ahead on the trail from the cave to the lake. At every twist in the familiar path, at every steep bit, they hurried a little more. Noticing all the familiar shrubs and rock outcroppings, Anneke rushed on, feeling her excitement mounting.

When they arrived at the small sandy and pebbly beach, Sheera ran straight to the water, tail wagging. Anneke looked around. When Mother was still at home in the trailer, this had been Anneke's place, to romp, to carve, or to get away. Over there was the tree branch she used to swing on. And to the left was the hole under the root where she stored food and later her carved animals. Now this was no longer her tree, her beach, her lake—it wasn't even called Fish Lake. All these places had been found by others. But Mother was gone—she still hadn't been found.

Anneke touched the little wallet with Mother's picture. Then, as she heard the adults arriving behind her, she turned and said, "Welcome to Lustre Lake."

"Fish Lake," Ken said.

"No. Lustre Lake." Anneke looked straight at him.

"OK," Ken shrugged. "But I like Fish Lake better."

"How lovely," Eileen exclaimed to Mrs. Bricks and Mrs. Uno. "I can see why you like to come up here."

"There's the fish trap." Ken pointed. "What's left of it." He, Larry, who had Elishia perched on his shoulders, and Anneke studied the remains of the stick and string structure.

"We'll take it down," Anneke said.

"No way, let's fix it," Ken protested. "It took almost a whole day to make it."

But Anneke shook her head slowly. "Nobody will come and get the fish that are caught. It's cruel to leave them swimming around until they die," she said. "And it will bring the bear back."

Larry liked the trap, but he agreed about taking it down. After they pulled out the sticks, Anneke made a tiny raft with some of the twigs and string. Using the bag they'd brought the apples in to keep her clothes and belt dry, she said, "Here, Sheera." Her dog took the end of the string.

"We'll be back," she called to the others on the beach.

"Where are you going?" Eileen asked.

As Anneke ran into the water, she heard Larry say, "They'll be fine," and she grinned. Catching up to the dog in a few strokes, she swam across the lake to the mouth of the creek. From there they walked to the huge tree that had hidden their grass socks until the searchers' dogs had found them. Anneke changed into her dry clothes and walked to the place where she had once, it seemed so long ago, spent part of a night in a storm. That's where the bed was, she thought. And over there was the branch that had held the wet bathing suit. She chuckled, thinking about the slimy thing that had attacked her.

"Come, Sheera." They sat on the old bed of needles. From her belt Anneke took the wallet with Mother's picture. "Things sure changed," she told the photo. "There are so many people in my life. Too many sometimes. I wish you'd come back. You're only a picture now. You're different. You always were different." She hugged her pet. "You and me, Sheera, we're still the same."

The dog licked her chin in answer. They romped on the ground, rolling around with each other in their familiar way. After a while they returned to the creek.

"We'll swim across Fish Lake for the last time," Anneke said. "From then on it'll be Lustre Lake."

When they returned to the beach, everyone had finished building a sand castle. They moved to a little fire Larry had made to roast hot dogs and marshmallows. They went for a swim, probably the last outdoor swim of the year, Larry said. Fall would officially start in a few days, although today was hot and summery. Elishia saw a big trout jump out of the water. She wanted to swim over to the spot and catch it. But Ken told her the fish had jumped up to catch an insect and would be somewhere else by now. They sat on the beach, drying their bathing suits in the late-afternoon sun and eating fruit and cookies. Birds sang in the trees. Here and there fish jumped, making rings in the glassy water. The sun's last rays of the day highlighted the greens of the evergreens and the golden leaves of birches.

Suddenly Sheera's ears pricked up. Ken thought he heard a noise in the bushes. Eileen grabbed Elishia. Larry told everyone else to stand on the beach behind the fire. Another rustling came from the bushes close by. Elishia started crying. Sheera's ears lay back. She growled.

Anneke saw a large stick, left where the fish trap had been. She ran over and grabbed it.

"Stay by the fire," Larry yelled at her.

The bushes moved. Jumping high in fright, a deer turned its white tail and crashed away from them, bounding into the forest. Sheera started to chase the animal, but Anneke called, "No!" Whimpering, the dog watched as two more deer rushed for the shelter of the trees a little farther down the beach.

"Look, Elishia—deer!" Mrs. Bricks said excitedly.

With the dog still whimpering, ready for a chase, everyone started talking at once. "This *is* wild animal territory," Larry said. "We'd better get dressed and pack up the rest of the food. It's time we headed back anyway."

Anneke picked up the little raft she'd made earlier and ran into the lake. Standing waist deep, she wrapped the string around the raft and threw it as far as she could. "Goodbye," she whispered. "I'll miss you." But Sheera swam out to the floating sticks and proudly brought them back.

"OK, dog, maybe we'll come here again someday." Anneke said, putting the raft in the hole under the tree root instead.

On Sunday afternoon a fine, chilly drizzle cooled the air. Gram and Grump came over for an adult game of cards while Anneke, Elishia, and Sheera watched a video. Gram came into the living room with a tray. "I brought something for my three girls," she said.

"*Three* girls?" Anneke said.

"Yes, you, Elishia, and Sheera. I made these myself. They're sweet." Gram put two blueberry tarts and a dog biscuit on the coffee table and left.

Biting into her tart, Anneke thought about the words "my girls." Sheera is mine. Elishia is Larry and Eileen's. Right now I belong to a photograph. But Mother *will* come back. She loves me.

After watching the rest of the video, they walked into the kitchen where the adults sat around the table. Elishia wanted "up" on Grump's lap.

"I'd like to phone Dr. Sunnybrook," Anneke said.

"Why?" Larry asked.

"I don't think Mother is really gone."

"I see the doctor at my work all the time," Larry said. "I'm sorry."

Anneke nodded. She wandered up the stairs to her bedroom. A rainy Sunday afternoon. Boring! She wound Mother's music box and looked at the photos in the old album. While winding the music box again, she saw Larry and Grump go into the garage. The card game must be over. "Long ago, long ago," the music tinkled. It *was* long ago that Mother had gone away, the night when she'd scattered the feathers in the trailer, the night she had been run over. Mother had left her first country, Holland, a really long, long time ago. She was different—she left. Anneke wanted to stay.

When the music box stopped turning, Anneke wound it once more, then, as she listened to the last of the tiny tune, she went downstairs. The music faded out. Voices faded in—Gram's and Eileen's.

"I agree," Gram said. "She has talent. She'll go far."

After a clatter of cooking pots Eileen said, "It's good to see her with Elishia. She's a real big sister to her. Elishia just adores her. The rest will all fall into place with time."

"I couldn't be more fond of her if she were my own," Gram said.

Anneke tiptoed back up the stairs. The music box had stopped playing. She didn't rewind it. Instead she drew a picture, a plan for a carving she'd make and leave on the coffee table someday. A picture of six hands placed one on top of the next, Grump's on the bottom, Elishia's on the top.

CHAPTER 11

Anneke dusted the carving of the six hands that stood on the side table by the couch. The wood had a new, second small crack in it, she noticed. The first one was caused by the stove's heat last winter, Larry had explained. The heat had dried the fresh wood and made it shrink. Now summer was here again and the second crack must be from the June sun shining hot through the window. She would ask Larry what to do about it. He had shown her the right kinds of wood to use for whittling since she'd made these hands. Last Christmas she had given the finished project to the whole family. They'd been so surprised and happy, and Eileen had even had tears in her eyes. Both Gram and Grump had given her a big bear hug, Anneke remembered.

A car drove up to the house. Probably a visitor for Eileen or Larry. The car door opened and a leg came out, then an arm.

"Dr. Sunnybrook!" Anneke threw down the

duster and rushed to the front door. She hadn't seen the doctor since she'd visited Mother in the hospital, a year ago. There must be good news about Mother. Or . . . Anneke pulled the door open.

"Hi," the doctor smiled. "Just the person I came to see."

The doctor looked happy, Anneke thought. "Hi," she said, smiling back. "Is it about Mother? Is Mother back? Is she OK? Can I see her?"

"I think the answer is yes to most of those questions," Dr. Sunnybrook laughed. "I have great news about your mother. Do you want to call Eileen and Larry? I'll tell everyone all at once."

Yes! The answer was *yes!* Anneke ran through the house. "Eileen, Larry, come quickly," she yelled up the stairs, then out the back door. The two adults rushed into the hallway, then stopped, their faces big question marks.

Dr. Sunnybrook smiled a greeting while Anneke yelled, "Mother's back. She's OK. Where is she?"

"Great news," Larry said. "Come in, Lucy."

"Wonderful." Eileen clapped her hands, then hugged Anneke, who could hardly hold still.

The adults took forever to come into the kitchen and sit down at the table. Finally, Dr. Sunnybrook told everyone that Mother had been brought back to a Vancouver hospital last night by a social worker. The worker had met Mother on the streets and started working with her while she was in a clear mind. First Mother had agreed to spend a few nights in a shelter for the homeless. Then the worker had persuaded her to check herself into the hospital. Mother was willing to be on medication regularly now, so the doctor had started a different kind of shots. So far everything was going very well.

"Will her schizophrenia be gone?" Anneke asked hopefully.

"No, dear," the doctor said. "It won't ever be gone. But right now she's in a good stage. She's not hearing voices. So we can work with her to control the illness. Things look promising."

"I'll find us a place to live," Anneke said. "I wonder—"

But Larry interrupted, "Let's hear the doctor out first."

Dr. Sunnybrook explained that Mother would be moved from the hospital to a group home, probably in the next couple of days. She needed to learn to take her shots and be with other people again after spending a year alone, mostly on the city streets. With good support she might recover completely and be able to lead a normal life, the doctor told them, although with schizophrenia you couldn't ever be sure and it was far too early to tell. Mother needed time. She also needed a lot of counselling.

Anneke's excitement came crashing down. This sounded just like before. "Can I at least see her?" she asked quietly.

"Oh, yes. Don't be discouraged," the doctor said quickly. "She asked about you. Your mother *wants* to see you! She misses you. That's a great sign.

Things are so much better than before."

Anneke brightened again. "When can I see her? Now?"

"Don't forget, your mother is in Vancouver. I haven't even seen her yet. A doctor there phoned me just this morning."

"We'll visit her; we'll find a way," Larry said.

"Absolutely," Eileen nodded.

"We were hoping to go slowly," the doctor said. "First we'll see if she can go to a group home around here. There's an opening coming up in a Nelson home. They have a good support group and we want to give everyone the best situation possible. Then she'd be close enough to visit."

"Sounds great," Larry said, playfully ruffling Sheera's head.

"Maybe your mom could phone you," Eileen suggested.

Anneke shrugged. "She's scared of phones."

Dr. Sunnybrook said, "A counsellor can try to help your mom understand that there isn't an evil voice coming from the phone. When she's no longer afraid of it, I'm sure she'll call you. That may be a while, though. You'll probably see her before then."

The doctor left with a promise to be in touch the next day, even if there was no news. Anneke hurried through the dusting, went upstairs, wound the music box, flipped through Mother's photo album, and skipped down to her workshop. With her new CD player booming, she whittled for a short while. But the piece, a neighbour's name carved onto the shape of a curved fish, was a big job. She needed to concentrate better. She walked into the kitchen, sat down, jumped up again.

"Why don't you go for a bike ride?" Larry suggested. "Ride over to Ken's."

She phoned him, then grabbed the new bicycle Gram and Grump had given her for her twelfth birthday and rode to his house. They packed a lunch and headed up to Lustre Lake. Sheera's tail wagged as soon as they reached the old cave. Anneke peeked inside, but the air felt damp and cold. The trail up to the lake was more noticeable this summer, since Mrs. Uno and Mrs. Bricks came up here regularly. They had cut some branches along the path and even dug out a few steps on the steep parts. Now Anneke ran to try to keep up with her eager dog. Ken followed slowly, which gave Anneke time to stand alone at her former refuge for a while.

"You were right, we did come back again," she said to Sheera, who ran right into the water.

The beach had been raked and cleaned. A small blue tarp hung from the big branch she used to swing on over to another branch. Under this covered area, in the shady spot, stood a white plastic table. An old cooler had been dug into the soil under the tree, its red lid propped open. A shovel, a rake, and two folded orange lawn chairs leaned against the tree. There was even a green mat in front of the cooler and under the table.

Ken arrived and looked embarrassed. "My mom and Mrs. Bricks did all this," he said. "They always fuss and clean."

"I guess the wild animals are gone."

"Yes," Ken said. "My mom never sees any signs of wildlife except squirrels, fish, and birds. But they always bring their CD player to let any animals know they're here."

"Let's swim across," Anneke said. "This isn't nature." She found the little raft still in the hollow under the root and tied their lunch to the sticks. Sheera remembered her job and took the string in her mouth.

"Let's just swim over there." Ken pointed to a nearby sandy spot. "It's not so far."

They left their clothes under the tarp and swam to a spot a little farther on. From there they walked along the shore a ways, swam again, and eventually arrived at the beach on the other side of the lake.

"Come and see where I spent the night once in a thunderstorm," Anneke yelled, running along the creek bed.

They made their way up noisily and soon found the big tree and the place where the bed of needles had once been.

"Cool," Ken said several times, looking around as Anneke told him about the branches that had crashed down around her and the hard rain that had fallen. They returned to the beach and ate their lunch.

While splashing Sheera, Anneke suddenly yelled, "Yippee, Mother is back!"

"Your mother? Back here?" Ken looked surprised.

Anneke had never talked to him about Mother's disappearance, about her illness. Now she said, "Last year my mother ran away. She has schizophrenia. That's why I'm living in a foster home."

"What's schis—whatever you said?" Ken asked.

"It's a problem with her brain. She can't always think the way most people do. She sees strange things and hears strange voices that aren't there. But now Mother's doing pretty good and she's coming back here. Yippee!" Anneke yelled, dancing in the water, feeling as light as a jumping trout.

Sheera barked excitedly. "Yes, dog. Mother's coming back. Mother. Mother!" Anneke called as the dog perked up her ears and looked around.

"Where will you live?" Ken stood on the beach, staring at her.

He has to be surprised, Anneke thought. But she didn't care who knew about Mother's illness. It wasn't shameful—she couldn't help it.

"I'll stay at my foster home," she said. "Mother will be in a group home."

"Oh, good, I like Mr. and Mrs. Proost, I mean Larry and Eileen. And especially Elishia," Ken said, relieved.

"Me, too," Anneke agreed. "I like them, and my workshop and Grump and Gram—Gram and Grump! They don't know yet! I have to tell them the news right now."

They headed back, walking and swimming along the opposite shore this time.

"That was fun, going right around the lake," Ken said. "Let's do it again."

Anneke agreed. They each found a bush to change behind and Anneke put the raft back.

"Next Saturday?" Ken asked as they walked down the trail. "It'll be the start of our summer holidays. My mom will be working, so she and Mrs. Bricks won't be up here. They only go together, he added.

"Maybe. I'll phone you tonight," Anneke said. She felt in a rush now, wanting to be the first to tell Gram and Grump the news, hoping Eileen or Larry hadn't told them yet. She rode straight past her own place and on to the grandparents', arriving tired and sweaty but not too out of breath to yell, "Gram, Gram, Mother's coming back!"

Gram was weeding a flower bed. With a huge smile she got up and rushed over, her arms out. "Finally," she said, hugging Anneke. "You knew all along she'd come back, didn't you?"

"Yes." Anneke said.

"Let's tell Grump and celebrate with ice cream." Gram wiped her sweaty forehead.

"Mother and Sheera and I used to celebrate this way too," Anneke said, setting a bowl of vanilla ice cream on the floor for the dog to lick. "We will again. When Mother is better."

"You'll have three homes to stay at then," Grump said.

"Maybe," Anneke hesitated. "Mother might have to stay in a group home for a long time."

"I look forward to meeting her," Gram said.

Going to the group home on the early July afternoon was scary, but Anneke insisted that she go alone. As planned, Dr. Sunnybrook met her at the front door at two o'clock.

"Your mom is well today," she said. "She's waiting for you in the rec room. Remember to be calm. That's easier for her."

They walked side by side, Anneke's hands feeling sweaty, her nails pressing into her palms, her feet trying to run to get there sooner. The door opened and there sat Mother. Anneke wanted to stand still and just look at the woman with the beautiful red hair. At the same time she wanted to rush over. Instead she walked beside the doctor, making herself stay calm.

Mother jumped up, then sat down again. She held out her hands. "Kindeke," she breathed.

"Mama." Anneke hugged her mother's bony shoulders, then sat beside her. "How are you doing?" she asked.

"Fine." Mother raked her fingers through her long hair, which had gone grey at the temples, Anneke noticed. She looked good, though skinnier than ever. And even though her eyes looked very sleepy, her face had a smile and she didn't shake as much. Only her hands moved a little.

"Did you bring some pictures, like we planned?" the doctor asked.

Anneke nodded. From her pack she took the photos she and Grump had sorted out for this visit.

"This is a picture of me and Grump and Gram." Anneke looked to see if Mother was paying attention. "They are sort of my grandparents."

"I always wanted for you to have a bigger family." Mother smiled as she studied the photo. "You look happy," she observed, sliding her arm around Anneke's shoulder.

"I am. I have so much to show you and tell you." They looked at the photos one after another, Anneke telling stories, Mother asking questions, making comments.

At the end Mother said, "I'd like to have a big picture of you to put in my room."

Anneke felt tingly all over. "Grump has lots of big pictures," she said. "I'll ask him. He even has videos of me at the GETT Camp and at Christmas and my twelfth birthday party."

"I'd like to see those," Mother said. "And Sheera too. How is she?"

Anneke talked about the dog, and Dr. Sunnybrook suggested a visit to Larry and Eileen's for the next weekend. When Mother told Anneke that she was learning how to play card games again and that she liked playing crib, Anneke knew the perfect solution.

"Gram or Grump and I play crib sometimes, on weekends," she said. "You can visit there. I'll bring

Sheera. Then you can meet them and see some of the videos Grump made."

Dr. Sunnybrook phoned Gram and arranged the visit. "But only for an hour," she said. "Gradually we'll make the outings longer."

When Anneke left the group home, Mother waved goodbye from the front steps. All the way back on her bicycle, Anneke felt herself smiling. Mother might still be sick, but she was better than she had been for a long time. Pedalling her bicycle faster with excitement, she said, "Sheera, wait until I tell you who missed you."

The week dragged on, but finally Sunday afternoon arrived. Anneke had checked that the video machine was ready, the cards and crib board were on the table, and the tea was made. When she looked out the front window yet again, Larry came driving up to the house. He had promised to pick Mother up and take her back. Mother would not meet Eileen and Elishia this time, because Dr. Sunnybrook felt that might be too much excitement all at once. "Things need to be really calm," she'd warned.

Mother looked beautiful in a new green summer dress with flowers that matched her red hair. She was shy when Anneke introduced Grump and Gram, but everyone smiled happily. Larry said he'd come back in an hour.

First they all sat down in the living room, where

Grump started the video so no one needed to talk. Gram brought in cups of tea and cookies. Anneke kept glancing from the video to Mother, who was looking closely at the TV screen, a smile on her face. From time to time everyone laughed when someone acted silly in front of the camera.

After watching for almost half an hour, Grump turned the VCR off. Anneke gave Mother a picture of her and Sheera in the Rockies. She said, "I have your Rockies photo album too. Would you like it back?"

"Yes," Mother said. "Maybe some day I will—no, *we* will go there together."

Then they played crib, Mother and Anneke against Gram and Grump. Of course Gram and Grump won big. And Mother dropped her cards twice, but Anneke didn't mind. She and Mother were at the same table, playing a game.

Just as they finished their second cup of tea, Larry came back. Mother climbed into the truck and waved at everyone.

"I'll see you next week," Anneke said.

"Yes," said Mother.

When the truck disappeared, Gram hugged Anneke. "A very good start," she said.

Anneke carefully carved the eye on the curved fish. The name plate for the neighbour was almost finished. She'd worked on the project off and on this week, between trips to the lake with Ken, an overnight stay at Gram and Grump's, and chores at home.

"Done," she sighed, setting the name plate on the workbench.

Sheera jumped up just as Larry called from the house, "Anneke, telephone."

It must be Ken. He phoned almost every day. She hurried to the kitchen where Eileen sat at the table, shelling peas, while Larry scrubbed potatoes at the sink.

Elishia noisily sucked juice from her cup. "Elephone," she said, a drop of juice running down her chin.

Anneke picked up the receiver. "Hi, Ken."

"Hello," came a soft, shy voice. "Anneke?"

"Mother! You're *phoning!*" Anneke yelled. Then she remembered Dr. Sunnybrook's words. *Always be calm. Stay calm no matter what your mother says or does.*

Quietly she said, "Mother, I'm so glad you phoned. This is Anneke."

"Is it really?" the voice came timidly.

"Yes, it is," she said. "I'm looking forward to your visit on Friday. We'll have a nice time. Don't forget to bring the cookies you promised to make."

"I'm baking them tomorrow." Mother's voice sounded more sure. "Are you really Anneke?"

"Yes, I am." And then she heard the words she'd been waiting for, the words Mother had said only long ago, before she'd gotten sick, the words Anneke had wanted to hear for so long.

"I love you, Kindeke."

"I love you too, Mama." Anneke said goodbye and listened for the click of the receiver as her mother replaced the phone. A look of pleasant surprise showed on Larry and Eileen's faces. She just smiled back at them, kneeled down, wrapped her arms around Sheera, and gave her an enormous hug.

photo: Val Swetlishoff

About the Author

An avid outdoors person, Ann Alma lives on a hobby farm in the Kootenay mountains with her dog, a border collie named Shira. She is the author of the award-winning *Skateway to Freedom* (in its fourth printing), *Under Emily's Sky,* and *Something to Tell.* Her books have received numerous awards including the Canadian Children's Book Centre's "Our Choice" award and two Silver Birch Award nominations.

Also by Ann Alma

SUMMER of **adventures**
Book Two of the Summer Series

Anneke stood with her back turned to the tree and scanned the area. She'd come from over there. No. Over that way. Actually, no, more to the right. ... Slowly the realization sank in. She had no idea where the river was: she was lost.

Twelve-year-old Anneke's dream of living with her mother seems an unlikely possibility. When her foster parents offer to adopt Anneke, she faces some difficult choices. Her struggle to decide where she belongs takes a new direction after she rescues a Japanese carving from a rushing river. The discovery leads Anneke and her friend Ken on an adventure in the beautiful, unforgiving Kootenay mountains. Lost in the wild, the two friends, accompanied by Anneke's dog, Sheera, must draw on all their strength and courage to survive. In the process, both Anneke and Ken discover what family really means.

Summer of Adventures
ISBN   1-55039-122-4   144 pages $7.95 Can $5.95 U.S.